A Hero for Her

A Curvy Girl Military Romance

Nichole Rose

D1713708

xoxo,

Nichole Rose

Contents

Dedication

To BOM – You never fight alone.

About the Book

The curvy songbird brings him peace. The broken Army Ranger gives her hope. But can love heal his haunted mind and save her life?

Ronan Gallagher

When I left the Army, I left behind pieces of myself.

The things I did haunt me. So do the friends I lost.

I thought I'd always be broken until I took a job protecting Winter Pyke.

This curvy songbird touches parts of me that haven't seen the light in years.

But a crazy fan has made her life a living hell.

That's a feeling I'm all too familiar with.

And I won't allow her to live the way I have for so long.

I will save her...and then I'm making her mine.

Winter Pyke

All I've ever wanted to do is sing.

I never expected it to come at such a high price.

The world knows my name, but I've never felt more alone.

Especially with a madman threatening to kill me.

Enter Ronan Gallagher, the former Army Ranger my manager hires to protect me.

I feel safe in his arms, and I'm falling fast.

But Ronan is fighting a battle of his own.

I've never been much of a soldier, but I want to be for him.

If he can fight for me, I'll fight for him too.

Chapter One

Winter

"Bartender, pass 'em around. Jack for me, Jim for my friends," I sing into the microphone, shimmying my hips and stomping my feet as the sold-out crowd sings along with us. "I'm on a mission to drown him out again. Line 'em up, we'll drink 'em on down. A shot to forget his whiskey voice. One to dry these amber eyes. Bartender, pass 'em around."

Gwen London dances along beside me, glowing under the bright lights on the festival stage. She's been on fire tonight. Then again, she usually is when we're on stage together. We've been headlining the *This is My Country* festival together for the last three months. I thought Riley Jamison was crazy when she asked me to headline with Gwen. Success is still new to me. Gwen is a freaking legend in Nashville. She burst onto the scene four years ago and smashed every record set in front of her.

Two years ago, I was a nobody, busking on the sidewalk and playing in bars between two part-time jobs and going to school full-time. And then Bentley and Cami Reynolds walked into the diner where I was playing. Within a week, I'd been signed with Riley Jamison's management company—Saunders Management. My life has been a whirlwind ever since.

It's impossible to feel like an imposter next to Gwen though. She's been amazing to me. If the whole world was whispering my name before the festival, they're shouting it now. I have Gwen to thank for that. She makes me look like a rockstar every night.

I launch into the last verse of the song, belting it out like I really know what heartbreak feels like. Unless losing the last piece of chocolate cake counts, I don't. But I've gotten good at faking it the last two years. I sing about love and lost love like I've been through both a time or two. But the only thing I truly understand is yearning, the desperate ache to belong...somewhere. To belong to someone.

I've been on my own for most of my life. Don't get me wrong. I have parents. They just cared more about appearances than they did about me. When I decided to pursue music, they couldn't get rid of me fast enough. Good girls don't run off to become big stars. They sing in the church choir. If I'm lucky, I hear from them every few months. Usually when they've seen me on the front of some gossip magazine and want to remind me that they're disappointed in me, my choices, blah, blah, blah. They never ask if what they read is true. I don't think they want to know that it isn't. The truth wouldn't suit their agenda and preconceived notions.

I belt out the last line of the verse and then launch into the final chorus with Gwen. She dances over to me and we sing into the same microphone, hamming it up for the crowd. They cheer and stomp, dancing along to the upbeat breakup anthem.

Sweat drips from my blonde hair, plastering it to my head. It's hot as Hades under the stage lights with so many people crammed into one place. Not even the breeze blowing through the outdoor arena does much to cool it down any. I sing the last notes, fanning my face.

Yeesh. Maybe I need to start training for marathons before I do tours.

"And keep them coming!" Gwen shouts, raising one hand in the air, as the band plays the outro and I reach for a bottle of water.

The crowd roars their agreement, making me smile.

"Y'all give it up for my girl, Winter," she says. "She may be five foot nothing, but the girl can sing her butt off, can't she?"

I blush when the crowd roars in response.

"These heels may look adorable, but they were not made for dancing," she says, kicking the red heels off. "My feet are killing me."

"I told you to wear boots!" her husband, Cyrus, shouts from the side of the stage, earning laughter and cheers from everyone close enough to hear him.

"As if I'm taking fashion advice from a man who wears exactly two colors," she sasses, smirking at him, which makes the crowd laugh again. "But you do make black look good."

Cyrus shakes his head at her.

I love them together. He usually has their twins, but since we're playing so close to home tonight, he left the kids with his sister so he could be here for her without having to wrangle two thee-year-olds. It's obvious how much he adores her. The way he looks at her makes me ache.

Everyone I know is happily in love—Olivia and Kasen Alexander, Addison and Clayton Devine, Gwen, Cami and Bentley, Riley and Cash Jamison. I'm the odd curvy girl out. I don't know why that's bugging me so much lately. I just feel...alone.

Even in a crowd of people, I'm an island. Everyone knows my name, but no one knows me. They know my music or who I'm wearing or where I've eaten. They want photos or autographs. They want to be seen with me. But very few want to know me. Those who say they do tend not to be the most stable of people. They send me creepy, inappropriate messages and letters. I have a whole stack of gross fanmail. It's exhausting, honestly.

"I'm going to sit myself right over there with that fine specimen of a man and have a drink," Gwen tells the crowd, pointing at Cyrus. "Winter has something special she wants to play for you tonight. When it's winning all the awards soon, just remember you heard it here on this stage first."

I gulp, butterflies kicking into flight in my stomach. I guess that's my cue.

I quickly set my water back down and grab my guitar before hopping onto the stool one of the stagehands runs out to center stage for me.

"I don't know about winning awards, but I do have something new I want to play for you guys tonight," I murmur to the crowd, plucking strings on my guitar. "This one is called *Cry*." I don't tell them what it's about or the story behind it. I just wait for them to settle down. Once a hushed silence falls over the crowd, I begin to hum.

My voice grows louder as the band joins me in a mournful tune that's far more blues than country. It's a haunting melody, one that fits the song perfectly. Gwen helped me fine-tune it. It's powerful and melancholy, exactly like the song.

I open my mouth to sing the first verse when...something in the crowd gets my attention. I'm not sure exactly how I see it or what I see, but the light hits the area just right, and a man dressed in all black comes roaring into focus. He's standing slightly apart from the crowd, a mask over his face. And he's aiming a gun right at me.

"Gun!" I cry, throwing myself off the stool onto my stomach.

A loud boom—like the crack of thunder—rolls over the crowd. My guitarist, Scott, cries out, doubling over as pieces of his guitar splinter off near his shoulder. I watch in horror as his white t-shirt immediately begins to turn red. He clutches the area, but the red area quickly blooms past his hand.

One thousand people scream simultaneously, chaos descending on the arena as another shot rings out. I scream too, placing my hands over my head to protect myself as best I can. My heart pounds, terror surging through me in a tidal wave.

I have to get off the stage. If I'm off the stage, whoever is trying to shoot me will stop. They won't shoot anyone else.

God, please let them stop.

I scramble forward, staying low to the ground as I try to get to the side of the stage as quickly as possible. Tears drip down my face, fear choking the breath from my lungs.

"Come on!" a familiar voice shouts. Hands grasp me, dragging me to my feet.

I sob as a wall of muscle surrounds me all at once. Cash Jamison, Bentley Reynolds, Memphis Hughes who plays drums for the band, and one of the record execs by the name of Dalton Grady. They grab me, curses flying, and charge for the side of the stage. Security rushes out behind them, yelling instructions at one another.

It's complete chaos backstage, as loud and frenzied as it was out there. But there's some semblance of order back here. People are taking charge. No, *Kasen* is taking charge. It's surreal to see him barking orders like a drill sergeant when he's usually the one Riley has to chase all over the place and threaten with bodily harm. Olivia and I are always laughing at him for complaining that she's terrorizing him. But he's got security running in every direction now.

For some reason, he isn't wearing a shirt. I'm pretty sure I don't even want to know why.

"Are you hit?" Cash growls, genuine fear in his eyes as he whips me around to face him. It's odd. I've never seen him or Bentley afraid before. They both look afraid right now, though.

For me? Because...because...I can't even let myself think it, let alone say it out loud. It's too awful. But I saw that gun. I saw it pointed right at me.

"Winter." Cash shakes me gently. "Focus, sweetheart. Are you hit? Were you shot?"

"N-no," I choke out. "No. But Scott..." A shiver wracks my body. "Someone shot Scott."

"I know." Cash's expression darkens. "They're taking care of him."

"I should help."

Do what, I don't know. The only thing I know about gunshot wounds is what I learned from repeatedly binge-watching Gray's. And I'm pretty sure that doesn't count as expert knowledge.

"Get her to her dressing room. Guard the fucking door. No one gets in unless my wife says so, are we clear?" Cash snaps to the group of men still surrounding me. A few security guards have joined the group, but the sheer size and reputation of the core four hold them at a respectful distance.

I don't think anyone wants to risk pissing off Cash or Bentley, and Memphis has a reputation himself. He used to be in an outlaw MC. Maybe he still is. No one really knows for sure. He won't tell us. And Dalton is Nashville royalty.

"Crystal," Memphis says.

"She isn't to be left alone until we find whoever this was," Bentley adds.

"It was a man," I mumble. "He was dressed in black and wearing a mask. I noticed him right after... Gwen!" I gasp, my heart slamming against my ribcage when I realize she isn't with us. "We have to find Gwen."

"She's safe, Winter. I saw her and Cyrus slip backstage just before you yelled gun," Bentley says. "She'll probably meet you in your dressing room."

"She's okay? You're sure?"

"I'm sure, sweetheart."

"Okay," I mumble, relief coursing through me. And then dread follows right behind it, sending bile crawling up my throat. "The fans. Was anyone else...?"

"I don't know," Cash says. "That's what I'm going to find out as soon as we get you to the dressing room with Riley and Cami."

I bob my head in a nod, too overwhelmed to say anything. I don't even know what to say anyway. Someone just tried to shoot me in front of a thousand witnesses. Who? *Why?*

I have no enemies. Heck, aside from the people here right now and their spouses, I don't have many friends, either. And my family wants nothing to do with me or my music. I'm just a curvy girl with a voice who got lucky. That's it.

But someone just tried to kill me.

"Come on, Winter," Bentley says, his voice both far away and too close as my teeth chatter. "Let's get you to your dressing room."

I nod again, ready to be anywhere but here. Right now, I think I'd rather be anyone but me.

Chapter Two

Ronan

"Get out!" I roar, running full tilt toward the group of soldiers standing in the middle of the overgrown village square. "Get the fuck out of there!"

Ericson turns toward the sound of my voice, scanning the mountainside for me. I wave my arms in the air, hoping like hell he sees me on the ridge. At this distance, my voice echoes, seeming to come from everywhere and nowhere at once. If any of it is audible to him, I don't know.

But I shout again, hoping like hell he hears what I'm saying. "It's going to blow!"

My lungs burn. So do my legs. I ignore both, pushing for more speed as I scramble over rocks, trying to get to my team before it's too late and the entire abandoned village goes up.

Ericson spots me, lifting his arm in a wave.

I fire off curses, spitting them toward the sky and whatever god is listening up there. If one is listening at all. I'm not so sure anymore. Not after two decades of serving in every hellhole known to mankind.

This one might be the worst. Nothing has gone right since we've had boots on the ground. Our radios are shot. The Somalian insurgents know we're here. My entire team just walked right into the middle of a village rigged to blow. And I'm too fucking far away to make a difference for any of them, a full mile of steep, rocky terrain still standing between us.

"Get the fuck–!"

The powerful blast rips through the village without warning, a fireball shooting skyward. The percussive blast knocks me off my feet. I land on my back, screaming in fury. In grief. In utter fucking helplessness.

Too late. I'm too goddamn late.

I come awake with a strangled gasp, sitting upright. My heart pounds a frenetic, sickening rhythm, pumping adrenaline through my system. Fight or flight locks every muscle in my body, demanding I do something...but there is nowhere to run, and no enemy left to fight. There hasn't been in two years. At least not for me.

"Fuck," I curse, scrubbing my hands down my face in an attempt to clear my head of the nightmare. It doesn't work. The sound of the blast still rings in my ears.

Wait. No. That's my phone.

I snatch it from my nightstand, dragging myself from the bed at the same time. My sheets are drenched with sweat. Same as every other night.

It's been two years since I lost my team in Somalia, and the memories of that day still haunt me. So does the week I spent in the mountains afterward, outnumbered, trying like hell to make it to the rally point with a group of insurgents on my six the whole way.

I'm still not sure how the fuck I made it out of there alive or how many insurgents I killed on my way down the mountain. I wasn't fueled by a desperate need to survive, but by pure rage. It's taken the better part of the last two years to work it out of my system. It took most of the first to heal from my injuries. Three gunshot wounds. A knife to the back. Exposure. A raging infection.

What didn't kill me damn sure didn't make me stronger. It took a year of physical therapy and a grueling exercise routine to get back some semblance of who I used to be. I'll never fully be that man again. I'll never serve again. The PTSD diagnosis ensured that.

"This is Ronan," I growl into the phone.

"Hey, brother," Elliot "Trick" Tricone says. "What's shaking?"

"Shit, brother." I blow out a breath, smiling despite myself. It's been a hot minute since Trick and I talked. We were in boot camp together a lifetime ago. He's retired Special Forces now. "It's good to hear your voice."

"Heard they finally let your ass come home from the program in California," he says quietly. "Welcome back, brother."

"Thanks," I mutter, striding my bare ass toward the bathroom. It doesn't feel like much of a homecoming, but there is no going back for me. PTSD is a bitch of a mistress. She's been kicking my ass ever since Somalia. Once I was discharged from the hospital, I went straight to a program in San Diego for soldiers like me, those who have seen and done highly classified shit and have the trauma to prove it. I've been there for most of the last year, trying to work through my shit.

"I know you're still settling, but Asher told me you were looking for work," Trick says.

"Shit, yeah," I say, stopping halfway to the bathroom. "If I have to stare at the goddamn walls, I'm going to lose my mind. I wasn't made for this shit."

Trick chuckles. "I feel you. They prepare us for war, not for what the fuck comes after."

"True story," I mutter. Fighting and killing and giving orders, I can do. Keeping people alive is what I'm best at. But sitting on my fucking hands all day, every day? I've never been good at that. Even as a kid, I sucked at it. And I joined up when I was eighteen. Been in since. Needless to fucking say, retirement is not off to a great start.

"A friend of a friend is looking to hire an around-the-clock bodyguard for a high-profile client, a musician," Trick says. "You been watching the news?"

"As little as possible. What musician?" I ask, my curiosity piqued.

"Winter Pyke."

Well, shit. I haven't been watching the news, but I wasn't born under a rock. Two days ago, someone tried to kill her while she was on stage. They shot one of her band members and caused a stampede at her show. It's hard to live in Nashville and not know about it since it's all anyone is talking about. Hell, it's hard to live in this town and not know her name. It's everywhere and for good reason. The curvy little songbird can sing her ass off.

"You interested?" Trick asks.

Interested? Fuck yeah, I'm interested. Every time I hear her voice, my dick is interested. There's something fascinating about her. Her amber eyes and shy smile make my heart beat a little faster when I see her pop up on the television. It's ridiculous because a man like me doesn't stand a chance with a girl like her. She's a superstar. I'm a washed-up former Ranger still sweating through nightmares every night.

But that's not what Trick is asking me.

"Yeah," I grunt, shaking my head to clear it of the bright-eyed little blonde songbird. "Yeah, I'm definitely interested."

"Can you be on Music Row in two hours to meet with her and her management team?"

Two hours? Guess I'm skipping my run and the gym this morning. And the stack of boxes in the other room still waiting for me to figure out what to do with them.

"If you don't think you're ready to tackle this, I can find someone else, brother," Trick says, misinterpreting my hesitation.

"I'm ready," I growl. "Was just trying to figure out what I need to accomplish between now and then. I just rolled out of the bed. I'm still bare-ass naked."

Trick chuckles. "Get your old ass in the shower. If she hires you, you'll be plastered all over the fucking papers. She's on every news channel and every gossip site in the country right now. Probably most overseas too."

"Jesus," I mutter. "Do they have any suspects?"

"Not that Kasen shared with Dane," he says, referring to his boss, Dane Robertson. I'm guessing Kasen is Kasen Alexander, the country musician. I don't know the full story, but Dane and Kasen's wife, Olivia, were briefly engaged a few years ago. She married Kasen and Dane married Sienna days later. Trick never shared the details, and I didn't ask. It's not my business. But I guess they still keep in touch. It's hard not to when you run in the same circles, I suppose. There are only so many billionaires in this state. "Says she's shaken up pretty bad though."

I shake my head, continuing into the bathroom. Poor girl is probably traumatized. Who can blame her? Being hunted is a hell of a thing. Out there in the mountains, I knew what I was facing, and it fucked with my head. I was trained for it. I spent two decades serving my country, and there were times when the mental exhaustion alone had me ready to just walk out into an open field and let them come and finish me off. I wouldn't wish that feeling on anyone, let alone an innocent girl like her. She isn't a soldier. She didn't sign up to fight a war or play war games. She's just a curvy little songbird, trying to chase her dreams.

"Text me the address," I growl to Trick. "I'll be there."

Less than two hours later, I pass through a throng of re-porters before pulling up to the security gates at Saunders Management on Music Row. Once the stressed guard fig-ures out who the hell I am and why I'm there, he waves me through, side-eyeing the crowd of reporters as if he suspects one of them may be the shooter. Hell, maybe one of them is. Wouldn't be the first time someone in the media tried to drum up a story by doing something completely mental.

The garage is virtually empty. I pull into a spot near the elevators just as two men and a petite woman step out of the stairwell. I recognize Kasen Alexander on sight. His mug has been plastered all over the place for long enough. The dark-haired giant beside him isn't nearly as famous but is just as recognizable. Cash Jamison, one of the biggest billionaires in the southern United States. Which means the curvy woman at his side is Riley Jamison, his wife. She's been making waves in this town for half a dozen years or longer.

They head in my direction.

"Ronan Gallagher?" Cash growls when I step from my truck.

"That's me."

"Hi," Riley says, holding her hand out for me to shake. She smiles, though she looks tense and stressed the fuck out. "I'm Riley Jamison. Thank you for meeting with us on such short notice."

I shake her hand and then quickly step back, not missing the warning look in her husband's eyes. He's territorial, possessive. I know better than to linger where I'm neither welcome nor wanted, and I'm neither of those things in his wife's personal space.

"This is my husband, Cash," Riley says, "and this is Kasen Alexander."

The three of us don't shake hands. We just give each other chin lifts. They're sizing me up, trying to decide if I fit in around here or if I can be trusted to guard Winter. They're protective of her, careful who they let close to her. That's a good sign. It means they're taking this shit seriously.

"Elliot says you were a Ranger," Cash says.

"Yeah. I was on an RRC team."

"An RRC team?" Kasen asks.

"A specialized recon team," I murmur.

"They're one of the most elite teams in the Rangers," Cash says.

Kasen eyes me with his head cocked to the side. "But you lost your whole team two years ago?"

"Kasen!" Riley hisses, smacking him across the chest.

"What?" he growls.

Riley glares daggers at him before turning to me. "You can ignore my idiot friend," she says apologetically, rolling her gray eyes like she's used to dealing with him saying whatever the fuck he wants to say. "He never learned manners."

"It was a valid question," he mutters.

Riley casually elbows him in the ribs. Hard.

He curses, doubling over.

"If he's going to be protecting her, I'd like to know that he's good too," Cash says quietly, though he's looking at me, not his wife. "Two years isn't that long after a loss like that."

"That's what I was saying," Kasen says.

Maybe the comment should piss me off, but it doesn't. It's a valid concern. Two years isn't that long. It's a lifetime and a mere blink at the same time, both far too long and never long enough. I forget their faces but never the charred remains of the village, the sound of their laughter but never the sound of the blast. No, two years isn't long at all. It's an eternity.

"I'm good," I mutter. It's mostly true. I've been through the program. I make it through every day without snapping. I'm not a danger to myself or anyone else. It's the nights that still fuck me up, those interminable hours when my subconscious takes over and I have to rewatch the whole damn day from beginning to end. There is no easy cure for those. No amount of group therapy or talking to a shrink to make them magically disappear. I know because I've been there and done that, over and over again. The goddamn nightmares still plague me.

Neither Cash nor Kasen looks entirely convinced.

"I was in the Army for twenty years," I say, crossing my arms. "I was a Ranger for most of that. I've been to every hellhole on this planet. I've trained with every elite fighting force there is to train with and know every weapon there is to know. More importantly, I know exactly what it feels like to be hunted and exactly how to avoid being captured. That's what I was trained to do. If there's a man in this state more prepared to protect your songbird than me, Trick would have sent them. He sent me because he knows I can keep her safe."

Cash and Kasen share a look and then Cash mutters a curse.

"You're the boss, little goddess," he says to his wife. "If you want to hire him, let's hire him."

"Actually, I'm not the boss this time," she says, giving me a small, apologetic smile. "It's up to Winter whether we hire him or not. She's the one who has to live with him. The choice should be hers. Let's go meet her." She spins on her heel without waiting for a response, marching back toward the entrance to the stairwell.

Cash sighs and follows after her, grabbing the door handle before she manages to get her hand on it. The hot look he shoots her makes it clear he's obsessed with her and her strong will. The adoration in her returned grin says she knows it and she loves him for it.

Kasen falls into step beside me. "Sorry if I offended you or some shit," he mutters, scrubbing a hand through his hair. "I didn't mean to bring up bad memories or be an asshole. We're just fucking worried about Winter. She means a lot to everyone here. She and my wife are close."

"It's all good," I say, not holding a grudge. I'd want to know the same information if our roles were reversed, though I'd probably have a few more questions. Actually, I have a few more right now, but I keep my mouth shut, figuring I'll get a chance to ask them later.

Kasen and I follow Cash and Riley into the stairwell and then through another door into the lobby of Saunders

Management. The building is nice...really fucking nice. A spiral sculpture stretches toward the roof of the building dozens of floors up, guitars of every shape, color, and design mounted carefully onto it. It looks almost like a Christmas tree, only one that probably cost a small fortune because every single guitar I set my eyes on has been signed by the artist who played it.

Unlike most buildings, the floors are hardwood instead of carpet. White leather furniture rests in groups around the lobby, with gold and platinum records hanging on the walls in neat rows. The front desk is shaped like a guitar, with *Saunders Management* written across the front in an elegant script. It's fancy as fuck.

But the most eye-catching thing in the room is the curvy little blonde pacing in circles beside the elevator. Six steps to the south. Five to the north. The heels of her ankle boots click against the floor with each step—*tap, tap, tap*—belying her nervousness. Her hair tumbles down her back in waves, swishing with every anxious step she takes. The hem of her little white dress shifts around her thick thighs.

I grit my teeth, groaning as my dick presses firmly up against my zipper at the sight of her. Even from an angle, she's more beautiful in person than she is on TV. She isn't just curvy. She's *thick*, her body soft and round, made to be held closed and fucked right. I can already imagine it. Her dripping sweat beneath me, her round cheeks flushed pink, and her eyes dilated with pleasure. Her teeth sunk into her bottom lip as she writhes beneath my touch, pleading for me to let her come.

Please, Ronan. Oh, please. Oh, please. Oh, please.

"Fuck," I mutter under my breath, stopping a good ten feet from her. If I get any closer, I'm not so sure I will stop. I'll put my filthy hands on her, and hands like these have no business touching a woman like that. It doesn't take a rocket scientist to see the innocence dripping from her. It's right there on her face, blazing like the sun.

No wonder Kasen and Cash are so protective of her. She's young and innocent. She probably has creeps crawling out of the fucking woodwork trying to be seen on her arm. Fuck all of them. They don't deserve her. Not if they don't treat her like a queen. And if they aren't standing here right now, roaring in fury because some motherfucker just tried to kill her, they clearly aren't worth the dirt on the heels of those pretty boots.

"You're too close to the windows," I growl when she paces within range of them this time.

She gasps and spins around, one hand over her heart.

Mine beats double-time, threatening to rip right in two at the sight of the tears still drying on her cheeks. *She's crying.* From eyes too goddamn bottomless to ever shed a tear.

New plan. I'm going to find whoever tried to kill her and end them.

Chapter Three

Winter

I know a thing or two about grief. I've become intimately acquainted with it in the last two days. And the giant standing ten feet away from me, feet planted apart, covered in tattoos and scars, is steeped in the corrosive bite of it. He hides it behind dark ink and a darker scowl, but the eyes never lie.

They tell a story I think he knows all too well. *Loss. Guilt. Pain.* His story is well-seasoned with all three. They glitter in the depths of his forest green eyes and tighten his severe expression. Even scowling, he's beautiful. Full lips and a sharp jawline beneath a neatly trimmed beard soften his expression, giving him dimension beyond simple severity.

He's an island in the middle of a storm. There's something calming about him, or perhaps it's the sheer size of him. Everyone feels small and vulnerable standing among giants like him. He's well over six feet tall, sculpted of thick, corded muscle. His size is the ultimate equalizer...something I've been sorely lacking for the last couple of days. I've been my own island, though I've been unmoored and adrift.

My friends have been amazing, don't get me wrong. But there's only so much they can do. They don't feel what I do. They aren't being targeted by a crazy man. They have their kids and their spouses and the assurance that, somehow, everything will work out. All I have is me. At the end of the day, they go home to each other. I go home alone.

I feel less like an island standing in front of this man than I have in a long time. He knows how I feel. I don't know what he's been through, but he's been through it. *And he's still standing.*

"Who are you?" I blurt, taking a step in his direction before I can stop myself. My hands ache with the desire to touch him, to trace my fingers down the lines of his tattoos until I understand the story they tell. Until I know his pain.

The black ones on his forearms...what do those mean? I think they're, perhaps, the most significant of all. Or whatever they're meant to cover are anyway. He blacked them out to avoid seeing them but didn't have them removed. He wanted the reminder that they're under there. Why?

"Winter, this is–" Riley starts.

"Ronan Gallagher," he growls, cutting her off. "You're still standing too close to the windows. Unless that's bulletproof glass, someone with a high-powered rifle could shoot you from the street or the building across the street."

My stomach churns at the thought, cold, hard fear slicing through me. I quickly move out of the line of sight of the windows, stepping into a small, recessed alcove between the elevators. "Better?"

"Yeah, that's better." He takes a few steps in my direction and then stops again. His green eyes scan me, his assessment meticulous. I think he sees me more clearly in these few seconds than anyone else has in years. "You holding up okay, songbird?"

"Winter," I whisper, acutely aware of the fact that Cash, Riley, and Kasen are watching the two of us intently. They don't say a word, but their silence speaks volumes. They're fascinated by the way we interact, though I don't know why.

"What?"

"My name is Winter."

"I know." Ronan stares at me for a moment, not speaking. He takes another step toward me before stopping himself again. "You're a tiny little thing. I thought you'd be taller."

"I am not short." I frown at him. "You're just tall. That's a *you* problem."

His lips twitch but he doesn't smile. He's very serious. Very somber. I don't think he smiles or laughs much. I doubt he has in a long time. "A me problem, huh?"

"Yes, as in you take it up with Jesus if you've got a problem," I mutter, trying desperately not to fidget like a nervous teenager. I feel like one standing in front of this man even though I'm twenty-two. My palms actually sweat, and my mouth is dry. I'm not even this nervous on stage.

"I'll do that, then," he says. I like his voice. He doesn't have a country drawl, but more of a soft growl. He doesn't speak loudly, but I don't think he needs to in order to be heard. His presence alone commands attention. "Do you know who I am, songbird?"

"You told me your name already."

He glances over his shoulder at Riley, who hurries forward with Cash at her side.

"Ronan is the bodyguard we talked about," she says. "He used to be an Army Ranger."

I glance from her to him. "You were in the Army?"

He nods.

Little pieces of his story begin to reveal themselves. The scars on his arms. The one along the side of his neck. The haunted look in his eyes. He's seen a lot. Probably more than he ever wanted to see.

"I know it's not always something you like to hear, but I was born and raised in the south," I say. "And around here, it's disrespectful not to honor the men and women who risk everything for us. No one deserves our gratitude and our respect more than you do. Thank you for your service, Ronan. The world is a safer place because men like you made the sacrifices you made to guard it."

Emotion flares in his eyes so bright it eclipses the sun. They blaze like twin pools of green flame, so darn bright they're blinding. "Thank you," he rasps, his cheek pulsing in a way that makes my chest throb.

My hands ache again, the desire to touch him nearly overwhelming. Not to satisfy my curiosity this time, but to offer him comfort. I think it's been a while since he's had any of that. I don't know what he faced or what he's endured, but it's clear it weighs on him.

"Why do you want to work for me?" I ask after a moment, trying to steer the conversation back to steadier ground for him.

"Because you need me."

I stare at him, not sure what to say in response to that. It wasn't an answer I expected. There's no arrogance in the statement, though, just simple statement of fact. He said what he means. He wants to work for me because I need him. Not because he wants something from me or because I'm a famous musician. Not because he wants to make it in Nashville and thinks I can help him get there. He's here simply because this is where he's needed. Because this is where *I* need him to be.

"He's the best man for the job," Riley rushes to say, mis-understanding my silence. "He worked for a special team in the Rangers. If anyone can help keep you safe, he can."

I nod, already convinced he's the right man for the job. "I guess my only remaining question is, when can you start, Ronan?"

"Now."

I blink at him.

"You need me now, so I start now," he says, shrugging.

"You know the situation?" I whisper, relieved they filled him in on everything and I don't have to go through it all over again. I've been over it a million times already. I just finished going over it with the latest detective sent to talk to me.

"I know some prick tried to kill you during the middle of your show two nights ago," he says, his expression dark. He doesn't like knowing I'm in danger.

My heart flutters at the realization before I frown at my friends. "You didn't tell him about last night?"

Kasen curses softly from behind him. "No. Figured we'd discuss it here in case the garage is bugged. You never know with the fucking paparazzi."

"What about last night?" Ronan demands, his eyes still locked on me. He hasn't looked away once, yet I bet if I asked, he could tell me more about the lobby than I could and I've been here too many times to count in the last two years.

"The concert was the first attempt on her life," Cash says. "But there was a...credible threat last night."

"A credible threat?" Ronan cocks a brow, silently asking what the heck that means.

When Cash and Kasen both clam up, hesitant to discuss the details when they freaked me out so bad, I sigh heavily and do it myself. "He means when I got home last night, someone had been inside my house," I say. "They left behind proof to document the occasion."

"Fuck," he growls. "What'd they leave?"

"Hundreds of pictures of me taped to the walls." I shudder at the memory. Walking into my bedroom felt like walking into someone's creepy shrine to me. My face stared back from every angle, image after image after image. Most were ripped from magazines or printed from my social media. But there were a few that were taken at concerts or around town. Those are the ones that really scared me. Whoever wants to kill me has been following me. They know me. That's utterly terrifying. "There was also a note."

"What did it say?"

"*What if thou withdraw in silence from the living, and no friend take note of thy departure*?" I wrap my arms around myself. It doesn't help defeat the pervasive chill I've felt since the festival. I doubt anything will thaw the icicles clinging to my veins until whoever is doing this is caught. "It's a line from *Thanatopsis* by William Cullen Bryant."

"Jesus Christ," he mutters, looking away from me for the first time. "The motherfucker knows where she lives?"

"Looks that way," Cash says.

"She can't go back there."

"I have to go home," I protest. "I have a cat and plants and a whole house."

"You can stay with us," Riley says, reaching out to squeeze my arm in sympathy.

"She can't stay with you," Ronan disagrees with a sharp shake of his head. "If he knows where she lives, you can safely assume he knows where the people closest to her live, too. She needs to go off the grid until he's caught, somewhere with no ties to her."

"Off the grid?" I gape at him like he's lost his mind. If he thinks I can just disappear until they catch this guy, he has lost his mind. "I can't go off the grid, Ronan. I have an album to finish and two more festival shows, plus a whole list of events I'm scheduled to attend in the next several weeks."

"Cancel them, songbird," he growls.

"He's insane," I splutter to Riley. "You hired a crazy person to protect me."

A menacing growl rumbles in his throat as he stomps forward, putting himself between me and my manager so I'm forced to look at him. "She didn't hire me," he says, his eyes locked on me. "You did because you know I can protect you. And protecting you means not dangling you like fucking bait in front of the psycho who wants to kill you, songbird."

"I can't just cancel everything, Ronan," I say, striving for calm. "I have a job to do."

"Is doing it worth your life? Because that's the risk you're taking."

I open my mouth and then snap it closed.

"If he knows where you live and how to get in undetected, chances are that he knows how to get access to you in the places you're most comfortable," Ronan says quietly, his green eyes boring into mine. "He knows you, Winter. Where you like to go, the things you like to do. Until they catch him or know who they're even looking for, you can't do those things."

"He's right," Kasen says quietly.

Cash nods his agreement.

Riley bites her bottom lip and then reluctantly nods too. "He's right, chica. As much as I want you out there doing what you do best, I want you safe more," she says quietly. "No one will judge you for canceling your appearances right now. Not with what just happened. If they do, screw them. They aren't your fans or people who matter. The ones who matter want you safe, even if it means you have to take a step back for a little while."

"What about the record company?" I ask, anxiety churning in my stomach. The last thing I want is to be targeted by a madman or to put anyone else at risk. But there are other people counting on me, like my band and their families. If the album doesn't happen because the record company decides we're overreacting, they don't get paid either. Neither do the producers or mixers or artists or dozens of others who go into making an album a reality.

"Leave them up to me," Riley says, her gray eyes steely. "I'll handle everything."

"God have mercy on Dalton Grady's soul," Kasen murmurs dryly.

Cash pulls a pen out of his pocket and hands it to his wife. Riley takes it without a word and sends it sailing over her head at Kasen, who barely manages to dodge it.

"What the fuck?" he mutters. "I was just saying that you're very persuasive. It's impossible to say no to someone with such a sunny disposition and a generous, loving spirit, Riley."

Cash snorts, earning a side-eye from his wife.

I watch the three of them, trying not to cry. It's their banter that sways me. If I stay and stubbornly go about my life like nothing has changed, it's them and their families I put at risk. After everything they've done for me, I can't do that to them. I *won't* do that to them. They're the closest thing to family I have anymore. I owe them so much.

"I'll do it," I whisper to Ronan. "Whatever you think I need to do, I'll do it."

Chapter Four

Ronan

"I can't even tell my band where I'm going?" Winter demands, glaring at me from the passenger seat of my truck. She looks pissed, but it's a front. She's clinging to her composure by the skin of her teeth. Anger feels safe. It's better than fear.

"The point of going into hiding is not to let anyone know where you are, songbird."

As far as the people in her world know, I don't exist. When we left Music Row, we left with her hiding on the floor of my truck. Riley drove off in her car, heading in the opposite direction. The paparazzi followed Riley. We drove around town for a while before we made our way to her house to pack her shit and grab her cat.

She didn't take long. As hard as she fought to go home, I don't think she really wants to be there right now. I think she just regrets the loss of the familiar. Everything she knew three days ago no longer feels safe. She no longer feels like she has control. Someone else took it from her. That's shaken her world on its foundations. I don't get the impression she's someone easily shaken. This little songbird may look soft, but she's a warrior underneath that angelic exterior.

"I thought you meant fans and the media," she mutters, her fingers flying across her phone screen again as she texts her band. "Not everyone."

"I meant everyone who doesn't absolutely have to know. As a matter of fact..." I pluck her phone out of her hand, jealousy eating me alive when I see Memphis Hughes' name at the top of the display. I don't want her texting her drummer. Maybe that makes me an asshole, but it's true. I want those amber eyes on me. "Do you back up to a cloud?"

"Yes. Why?"

I hit the automatic button for the window and toss her phone.

"Ronan!" she shouts, lunging toward me too late to save it. "What are you doing? Are you insane?"

"They can be traced." I let the window up again, leaving her phone in pieces on the side of the highway. Now, she's mine. Fuck. I mean her attention is mine.

"You...you..." She flings herself back against the seat, so mad I'm surprised steam doesn't come rolling from her ears. "I can't believe you just did that."

"We'll get you a new phone, songbird. Something that no one else has had their hands on." Preferably after I've had her all to myself for a few days because the more I think about having this girl in my space, the more I like it.

The longer I spend around her, the more I want her. She's fascinating to me. Not because of who she is—I don't give a fuck if she's a country musician or if she works a cash register at the gas station. There's just something in those eyes that captivates me, something that demands I protect her at all costs. That I claim her no matter what. It makes no goddamn sense to me.

I've never dated much. In fact, I can't remember the last time I went on a date. Chasing pussy was never something that interested me much. Too many one-night stands end up with lasting consequences, like kids that weren't planned. Doing the shit I did for the Army...well, the last thing I wanted was to get some random woman pregnant knowing I might leave a kid behind. So I kept my dick in my pants where he belonged. It was easy enough to do.

But the desire to touch Winter is damn near a compulsion at this point. I want my hands on her. I want in her space. I want to leave reminders of myself on her delectable body. Every time I look at her, fifteen competing desires war for dominance, urging me to take and claim and glut myself on her. It's fucking with my head because the last thing she needs right now is some asshole in her personal space, trying to lay claim to her. But that's precisely what I want to do anyway.

"What did you do for the Army?" she asks.

"Recon."

"Was it classified?"

"Almost always."

"Were you in charge?"

"I led a team."

She nods as if this answer satisfies her. "That explains so much," she mumbles, making me smile despite myself. "You're bossy and paranoid. What kind of recon did you do?"

"The classified kind."

She growls at me, making me smile again.

"You should do that more."

"Do what?" I ask, glancing from the road to her.

"Smile," she says. "You should smile more." She peeks up at me from beneath her lashes. "It looks good on you, Ronan."

"Haven't had much to smile about for a while, songbird," I admit, turning back to the road.

She sighs softly from beside me. A moment later, I feel her small hand slip into mine on the center console.

"Me either," she whispers.

"It's not much," I mutter, dragging a hand over my short hair as Winter wanders around the bedroom across the hall from mine. Compared to her place, this place is a hovel. It's a two-story Craftsman in the woods. There isn't much around but nature and silence. Her place is a McMansion in one of the nicest neighborhoods in Nashville, complete with a pool and a nice view of the city. But my place offers what hers doesn't. Safety.

"You haven't been home long," she says, glancing up at me from the stack of boxes in the corner.

"Just got moved in two weeks ago."

"You were deployed?" A faint smile dances at her lips. "Doing recon?"

"No. I was in California."

"I like California," she says, that sweet smile growing. "The ocean is always so peaceful to me. Standing on the beach staring into the immense vastness of it always puts things into perspective for me. Me and my problems seem small in comparison." She laughs, brushing hair back from her face in an endearing, self-conscious gesture. "That probably seems silly."

"Not at all." I lean back against the wall, my arms crossed as I watch her wander around, examining everything in the room. There isn't much—a small desk, the bed, a night-stand, and a dresser. A bookcase in the corner holds a stack of old books that came with the house. Everything smells new and fresh, as if the oak furniture was freshly right before it was delivered.

"Were you stationed in California?"

"No." The word comes out harsher and more abrupt than I meant.

"I'm sorry." She glances at me over her shoulder, her lip caught between her teeth. "I didn't mean to pry."

Shit. Now she thinks she upset me.

"I was in a treatment program for PTSD, songbird," I say bluntly. Might as well get that shit out of the way now. I don't want her thinking she has to walk on eggshells around me or that she can't ask me questions. If she's going to live here, I want her to be comfortable. I want her to feel at home. I want...Christ Almighty, I want *her*.

"Oh, Ronan," she whispers, striding across the small bedroom toward me. "Now I really feel like a jerk. I keep bringing it up, and it's probably the last thing you want to talk about."

"You aren't a jerk," I growl. "I don't have any secrets, Winter. Anything you want to know, you ask me. You might not like the answers, but I'll give them to you."

She eyes me for a moment, her amber eyes scanning across my face. "Why?"

"Because you need to know that you can handle this shit," I say, reaching out to touch her cheek. I can't fucking help it. She's standing in front of me, soft and sweet and vulnerable, and I need to touch her, just to see if she's real. Just to see if she's as soft as she looks. A spark jumps from her skin to mine, plunging all the way to my fucking soul. "You need to know that you aren't alone and this motherfucker won't win."

She sighs softly, stepping into my touch. "I'm tired of feeling alone."

"You aren't alone," I growl. "Not anymore, songbird. I'm right here, and I'm going to get you through this, all right?"

She nods, blinking back tears.

I curse silently and drag her into my arms, She comes willingly, allowing me to wrap myself around her. I hold her tight, taking as much comfort from her sweet embrace as I give to her. She's the sweetest thing I've ever had in my arms. And she smells like peaches.

"I don't feel so alone anymore, Ronan," she whispers into my chest.

"Good because you aren't."

She tips her head back to look up at me, her amber eyes wide and somber. "Neither are you, you know. I don't know what you went through or what you're still going through. Maybe you don't want to talk about it with me. But I'm here," she says. "If you ever want to talk, I mean. I'm here."

How can this tiny, brave little songbird stand beneath the weight of what she's going through and offer to bare the weight of my pain for me too? I don't know. Is it possible to fall in love in the blink of an eye? If so, I think I just did.

"I lost my team in Somalia two years ago," I murmur. "We were looking for a village of hostages to carry back coordinates for a strike team, and everything went wrong. A group of al-Shabaab insurgents spotted us and rigged an old village to blow. I was lagging behind, trying to get a signal on our radios when I heard their transmission. By the time I got close enough to warn my team, it was already too late."

"I'm so sorry," she whispers. "I can't even imagine what you went through."

"Hell," I rasp. "I went through hell."

She squeezes me as if she intends to mold me back together through sheer force of will alone. "Thank you for telling me."

I lean down, brushing my lips across hers in a soft, grateful kiss. "Thank you."

"For what?" she whispers.

"For being you, Winter." I step back, determined to give her a little space before I push too far and take too much too soon. "Why don't you get settled in while I go make some calls and see if I can't get some people on your case?"

She blinks those big, beautiful eyes at me. "You can do that?"

"Baby, you didn't just hire a bodyguard. You hired the pushiest motherfucker this side of the Mason-Dixon. If I can survive three bullet wounds and a knife in my back in the middle of the goddamn mountains in Somalia, you better believe I can light a fire," I growl, turning for the door.

She grabs my arm. "You were shot three times?"

I lift my shirt, showing her the silvery bullet wounds and scar tissue littering my torso.

"Ronan," she gasps, reaching out with trembling fingers to trace the worst of the wounds.

I groan, my cock imprinting against my zipper and pleading for relief at the feel of her hand on my abdomen.

She immediately jerks her hand away, jumping as if I burned her. "I'm sorry." Her cheeks blaze with color, her gaze bouncing around to keep from meeting mine. "I shouldn't have done that."

No, she shouldn't have. Because now I'm pissed she stopped. I want her hand back on me. Only I want it lower this time, wrapped around my cock while she sucks on the fat head.

Jesus Christ.

"It's fine," I growl, stomping from the room before I snatch her up and do something I can't take back. Like fuck her up against the wall.

Fuck my life. There's no way I'm going to be able to keep my hands off this girl. None at all.

Chapter Five

Winter

"Get out of there," Ronan groans from across the hall. "It's going to blow."

My heart clenches in my chest, threatening to crack in half. He's dreaming about the day he lost his teammates again. He had the same nightmare last night. I know because I spent half of the night standing vigil outside of his room, trying to keep him company. I don't know why. I just didn't want him to be alone while he suffered through the nightmares, but I wasn't sure if I was allowed to intrude, either.

I can't listen to him suffer in silence again tonight, though. Last night was hard enough. He's still in so much pain, still haunted by things I can't even imagine. He spent most of today on the phone, making calls to try to help me.

But the whole time, I couldn't help but wonder who fights for him? Who protects him? I have a feeling the answer is no one. He really is an island, fighting the storm on his own.

"Not anymore," I mutter, flinging my blankets back and climbing from the bed. I've never been much of a soldier. I know nothing about war. I'm barely keeping my head above water in my own battle. But if he can fight for me even through his, I'll fight for him through mine, too.

Tuesday lifts her head and meows at me in protest before closing her eyes again, too comfortable to move. She's a senior cat, far past her prime. I found her while I was busking downtown three years ago. She'd jumped into a trashcan in search of food and couldn't get out again. I brought her home with me and she's been with me ever since.

I pad toward the door to my room and slip out, pacing across the hall. A floorboard creaks faintly halfway between my room and his. It doesn't wake him though. Neither does the door opening. I stand in the doorway for a long moment, my eyes locked on the bed.

He's naked, moonlight spilling in from the windows and the skylight over his bed. The sheets are twisted around his powerful body like ropes holding him to the bed. He's restless, shifting this way and that as he fights the memories plaguing his sleeping mind.

"Ericson," he mumbles. "Goddammit, Ericson."

I push his door closed and cross toward him. "Ronan."

"Ah, Keller," he groans, his expression contorting. "I'm sorry. Christ, I'm sorry."

A tear slips down my cheek.

"Ronan." I reach out, placing my hand on his arm to shake him.

As soon as my palm makes contact with his arm, his eyes pop open. For a long, silent moment, he stares right through me, still locked in the nightmare haunting his mind. And then he groans, a devasting, heartbreaking sound. He sits straight up, his hands encircling my waist as he yanks me toward him.

I topple onto the bed, landing on my back beside him. He rolls, coming down over me.

"Songbird," he breathes, his face shadowed from this angle. One shaking hand touches my cheek, his fingertips gentle as they collect the wetness there. "You're crying."

"You were having a nightmare. A bad one," I whisper.

He falls still on top of me, his gaze searching across my face. "You were crying for me?"

"Yes."

He whispers my name so softly I barely hear it, and then his lips are on mine. He doesn't kiss me sweetly, a mere brush of his lips like yesterday. He kisses me as if he needs me to survive. The groan that vibrates from his lips is so full of desire, of desperation that it pulls an answering moan from somewhere deep in my chest. The ache I've felt since he touched me yesterday comes roaring back to the surface, hotter and hungrier than before. I moan again, reaching for him with both hands.

"Fuck," he growls against my lips, yanking my thigh up over his hip.

I gasp his name as his erection grinds against my clit, sending shockwaves through my system. I've never been touched there, let alone felt anything like him right there. He's hot and hard, his desire potent as he consumes me in a scorching kiss.

"Tell me to stop," he growls, breaking from my lips to kiss a hot trail down my chest. His teeth close around my nipple, pulling a sob from my lips.

"Don't stop," I sob, clawing at his strong shoulders. "Oh, God, Ronan. Don't stop."

He growls my name, sucking my nipple into the hot cavern of his mouth through my camisole. One rough hand glides down my body, yanking my shorts and panties to the side. His fingers brush across my wet slit.

"Tell me to stop," he growls again. "Goddammit, songbird. Tell me."

"No." I drag my eyes open, meeting his in the dim light. "Don't stop, Ronan. Don't ever stop."

He roars a curse, ripping my camisole right down the middle. I sob his name, tangled so tightly in a net of desire, I can't catch my breath. I can't think. All I see, all I feel is him. And I desperately want more. I need more.

He slips his erection between my legs, pumping his hips so the head of it drags against my clit. I sob in ecstasy.

He growls, falling forward onto his forearms as he attacks my breasts with that wicked mouth. He nips and sucks, leaving a trail of love bites littered across my skin. "These perfect little nipples," he growls. "Goddamn, songbird. I could suck on them all fucking night and still not be satisfied."

"Ronan!"

"You want more?" he demands, reaching between us again. He grabs his erection, pressing the head of it against my hole. "Stay still, songbird. Let me put the tip in. Just the tip. Fuck, I need to feel you around my cock when you're coming on me."

Oh, my god.

"I...I..." I start to tell him that I've never done any of this before but the words get lost somewhere between my brain and my mouth when I feel the head of his erection breech my opening. I writhe beneath him, moaning his name.

"You like that, songbird?" he whispers, panting against my ear. "Fuck, your hot little cunt is already strangling my cock." He pushes the head into me and then back out, both of us groaning. Both of us writhing.

"More," I plead. "Please, more."

"No."

"Please. Oh, please. Oh, please." I scratch down his back, not above fighting dirty to get what I want right now. I want him in me, satisfying the ache deep inside. I need him inside to satisfy it. Nothing else will suffice.

He curses, pushing the head of his cock inside me again. "Stay still," he growls, grabbing my hip in one hand. He reaches between us with the other, grinding his thumb against my clit as he presses his lips to my ear. "Be a good girl and come on my cock just like this, songbird. Don't make me spank your pussy to get what I want."

"Ronan," I sob, shocked and turned on by the filthy, dominant way he speaks to me, as if my body is his to do with as he pleases. As if he's in charge here and my only job is to take what he gives me. I like it a little too much, I think.

"Come, songbird," he rasps. "Right fucking now." He delivers a sharp bite to my lobe, grinding against my clit at the same time.

The combination of pleasure and pain sends me catapulting over the edge into an orgasm unlike anything I've ever felt before. I shout his name, my muscles locking up tight as I shatter apart in his arms. My heart pounds, the whole world lighting up in a kaleidoscope of color.

"That's it," he croons, sitting back on his heels. "Just like that, songbird. Fuck, I'm barely in you and that tight cunt is strangling the head of my cock."

I feel him moving and peel my eyes open. Another aftershock rips through me when I see his fist wrapped around his thick shaft. The head of his cock is still inside me as he jerks himself off into me, his eyes riveted on where we're connected. He looks so beautiful in the moonlight, so fierce.

"Ronan," I whisper.

His gaze flicks to mine, a grunt leaving his lips as his body tenses.

I writhe in ecstasy beneath him as he comes, spilling inside me in warm spurts that leave me trembling. He keeps his eyes locked on mine, holding my gaze captive the entire time, as if daring me to look away or deny what he's doing. I don't. I can't.

He falls still, his eyes still locked on mine as he pants for breath.

I lick my lips, staring at him in silence.

He groans, pulling out of me. I bite my lip, hating to lose his heat. His cum drips down the crevice of my ass, making me squirm. He notices and something predatory flares in his eyes. He drags his thumb through my slit, still watching my face.

"This belongs inside you, Winter," he says, pushing his thumb inside me.

My core clenches around his finger, another aftershock tearing through me.

He grunts in satisfaction and falls beside me, dragging me into his arms. His lips brush my temple in a soft kiss. "Don't cry for me, songbird," he says after a moment. "Cry for the men who didn't make it home. They're the ones who deserve your tears."

"So do you," I whisper, burrowing into his arms. "I'll cry for you if I want to cry for you, Ronan. My tears are mine to shed how I see fit."

"Feisty," he says, the hint of a smile in his voice.

"I decided something."

"Yeah? What's that?"

"If you're going to fight for me, I'm going to fight for you."

"Oh, yeah? You're going to be my white knight, Winter?"

"No. I'm going to be the reason you sleep at night," I say. I don't know much about PTSD, but I know enough to know that a lot of people find it easier to sleep next to someone else than they do to sleep alone. He didn't necessarily invite me into his bed, but he did put me in it. I figure that's close enough to the same thing.

"Fuck," he rumbles, rolling us until he's looking down at me again. "You're dangerous, you know that?"

I frown up at him, not sure what he means by that. "How so?"

He brushes strands of hair back from my face, studying me intently in the dim light. I can't read his expression well, but it's soft. "You make me want to keep you," he murmurs. "But you weren't made for a cage."

"Who says you have to keep me in one?" I whisper back.

"I talked to the lead detective on your case," Ronan says, setting a heaping plate of bacon and eggs in front of me the next morning. How he expects me to eat it all, I don't know. But it looks delicious.

"What did he say?"

"He had a lot to say," he says, grabbing his own plate from the kitchen before crossing back to the table. He sets it across from me, looks up at me, and then scowls and circles around to my side of the table. He drops his plate in front of the chair beside me, pulls it out, and takes a seat, but not before moving it as close to mine as possible.

I shovel a bite of scrambled egg into my mouth to hide a smile.

We fell asleep cuddling last night. He didn't have nightmares again. At least none that woke him or made him restless. He seemed to sleep peacefully. We didn't wake up until nearly nine this morning. He seemed shocked to have slept so long.

We didn't talk about what happened between us last night. But he kissed me before he crawled from the bed and dragged himself down to his home gym. I occupied myself with writing a new song or trying to write one. It feels more personal than anything I've ever written before now, more real. I'm still fine-tuning it.

"The most important thing was that he believes whoever is responsible is someone you're familiar with," he says.

I stop chewing to look at him. "Someone I know?"

He nods, his expression grim. "They've been going through the threatening fan mail you've received. There are a few letters that raised some red flags. Anderson thinks they're from the same guy."

I set my fork back down on my plate, suddenly far less hungry than I was two seconds ago. "Why does he think they're from the same guy?"

"Scripture." He takes a swallow of coffee. "Several of the letters reference scripture. I haven't seen them, but he said most of them are written in a threatening context. Do you know what he's talking about?"

I nod reluctantly. "I started getting them about a year ago, right after I performed at the Grammy's. I assumed they were from some preacher who was upset about my performance. I don't really know anyone..." I trail off, a disturbing thought crossing my mind. My parents are heavily involved in a church of sorts. It's more of a cult than anything, truthfully. They have been for most of my life. It's part of the reason my parents were always so deadset against me pursuing music as a career. But my dad doesn't believe nearly as strongly as my mom, and my mom wouldn't do something like this. She wouldn't try to kill me. She barely even speaks to me. Besides, my mom is tiny. The guy who tried to shoot me wasn't tiny.

Brother Gibbs isn't though, a little voice whispers in the back of my mind. I immediately push it away, refusing to even entertain it. The pastor of my parents' church might send letters condemning me, but why would he try to kill me? What purpose would it serve?

"What?" Ronan asks. "What was that thought?"

"It was nothing."

"Liar," he says, his eyes narrowed on my face. "You thought of someone."

"I didn't," I lie.

"Don't lie to me, songbird. I can't help you if you lie to me." His dark green eyes glitter, his expression severe. "And it'll just piss me off if I have to find the answer myself."

I scowl at him, annoyed at how freaking bossy he is. "I thought I hired a bodyguard," I mutter. "Not a freaking drill sergeant."

"Well, you got both. Deal with it, baby." He hooks his foot around the leg of my chair, dragging it around to face him. "Who did you think about that you don't want to tell me about?"

"My mom," I growl. "I thought about my mom, okay? But I know it wasn't her because I saw those letters and she didn't write them. And I saw the person pointing a gun at me and it wasn't her. She's shorter than I am. He was a lot taller, and he was built like a man."

He stares at me in silence for a moment, not blinking. "You aren't close with your mom."

It's not a question.

"My parents don't approve of my career choice. Music was fine when I sang in the church choir, but once I quit college to pursue a career, they made it pretty clear they didn't support me or my choices," I say, staring at the table. Good girls don't make spectacles of themselves. They serve the church and the family and lead simple lives. They don't run off to Nashville. They don't wear tiny dresses and sing inappropriate songs. I'm an embarrassment to them because I didn't confirm.

"Jesus," he growls, plucking me out of my chair. He plops me down in his lap, tilting my head back until I'm forced to meet his gaze. "You deserve better, songbird. I'm sorry."

"It is what it is," I say quietly, my heart pulsing at the softness in his expression. "I learned quickly that not everyone who should support you does, and not everyone who says they're in your corner actually are. It comes with the territory when you're in this business."

"That's fucked up."

"That's Nashville."

"It's fucked up," he says, enunciating each word carefully. "You deserve better."

He's right, but my parents are who they are. They aren't going to change just because I wish they would or just because their behavior hurts me. My parents think Nashville is one step from Los Angeles, and Los Angeles might as well be parked outside of hell's front gates.

"Regardless, it's not my mom," I say and then laugh abruptly. "She's probably pitching a fit about how mortifying it is to have me all over every news channel in the country right now. It'll have the old ladies at church gossiping for weeks. She'll hate that."

Ronan grunts, though I'm not sure if the sound means he hopes she is stewing in her own juices or if it means 'eff her and the pony she rode in on. It's hard to tell with him. He expresses a lot through grunts, but they sound a lot alike.

"Finish your breakfast, songbird," he murmurs, pressing his lips to my temple.

"Are you going to put me back in my chair first?"

"Nah." He grabs my plate, dragging it closer to his. "I like you right where you are."

Chapter Six

Ronan

"You want to do what?" I growl, glaring at Winter across the living room.

"Go to the hospital to visit with the fans who were hurt at the show," she says calmly. "And before you get all grumpy and tell me no, you should know that this isn't something that I should skip nor is it something I want to skip. If I don't show up to visit, it will destroy their faith in me."

I stare at her placidly, tempted to tell her hell no regardless of what she wants. The last place she needs to be is at the hospital visiting with fans, one of whom just tried to kill her. But after our conversation this morning...I'm no longer convinced it was a fan. She's sure it wasn't her mother, but I'm not as convinced. I just need a little time to do some digging. If her parents are as religious as she says, it's very possible it is one of them, as much as she doesn't want to consider it.

"This is important to me, Ronan," she says quietly. "I'm where I am because they supported me. They showed up at my shows and bought my albums. And now they've been hurt because someone tried to hurt me. It's not just insensitive to ignore that, it's cruel. They deserve better from me. I know it's risky, but some risks are worth taking."

"They mean a lot to you, don't they?" I ask, softening slightly.

"Yes." She nods emphatically, her ponytail bobbing with her head. "It's hard to be a curvy girl in the music business. Even in this day and age, everyone still has something to say about the way we look and the way we dress and how much we weigh, and how fat our butts are. God forbid if we're photographed eating or if we don't love the gym or have a personal trainer. The media loves to criticize us for being human and having human bodies," she says. "My fans are the first to shut that crap down."

I stomp toward her, growling. "People say mean shit about you? They talk about your body?"

"Uh, only every day." She rolls her eyes.

"Who?" I demand, stopping in front of her. "I want names, songbird."

She tilts her head back, looking up at me. A tiny smile curves her lips up at the corners. "Why? Are you going to go knock heads for me, Ronan?"

"I was thinking more along the lines of sticking my boot up their asses until they feel my toes tickling their tonsils," I mutter, wrapping my hands in her shirt to pull her toward me. "But yeah, same principle."

"That may be the sweetest thing anyone has ever wanted to do for me," she whispers.

"I'm your bodyguard, songbird. That means it's my job to guard this fucking perfect body." I tug her forward until she's pressed up against me, her luscious tits against my chest. "No one talks badly about you or makes you feel like anything less than the goddamn knockout you are unless they want to deal with me."

Her expression goes soft, her amber eyes practically glowing. "You think I'm a knockout?"

"You think I was jerking off into that cunt last night just because you were there, Winter?" I ask, cocking a brow at her. "Hell no. You're the prettiest little thing I've ever seen. My dick hasn't gone down since I saw you. I don't know what the hell you see in a man like me, but I'm not questioning my good fortune. So long as you want me, I'm not telling you no."

"What if..." She peeks up at me through her lashes. "What if I'm not ready for this to end when I no longer need a bodyguard, Ronan?"

"Then it doesn't end," I growl, palming her ass. "But I hate to break it to you, songbird. You need a bodyguard permanently. There are too many fucked up people in the world willing to do shady shit to get close to you. You need someone with you to guard your privacy and your personal space." I have a feeling she isn't good at doing that herself. Her heart is too big.

She hasn't learned how to guard it or how to tell people no yet. She feels like she owes her fans too much. I'm guessing she lets them stop her on the street or in the grocery store or in the bathroom for photos and autographs and a minute of her time. It's why everyone around her is so protective of her. They know how much of herself she gives to her fans and everyone else.

"I'll think about it," she says.

"Good. Let's go to the fucking hospital before I change my mind."

"Now?" She blinks at me. "You want to go right now?"

"Yep," I say. "We're not giving anyone a warning that we're going, songbird. I don't want it to leak to the press or anyone else until we're already there and visiting. This should be a private moment between you and your fans." Hopefully, one where she's safe, and whoever the fuck is trying to kill her has no idea she's tiptoed out of hiding until she's already on her way back here, satisfied that she's done her duty to her fans.

We're not at the hospital long before word begins to spread that she's there. Within half an hour, a small throng appears, trying to get photos and her autograph as she moves from room to room, checking on the fans still hospitalized.

The throng stretches across the hallway, completely blocking it. The noise is overwhelming.

Winter shrinks in on herself when she sees them, her anxiety soaring. Mine does too.

"Go on ahead, songbird," I murmur to her, nudging her toward a young fan's room. "I'll deal with this."

"Be nice," she scolds me, worried about her fans even though she's anxious about the crowd.

"I'll be sweet as pie."

She doesn't buy my bullshit for a minute, but she reluctantly heads into the hospital room, leaving me to deal with the throng at the end of the hall. I stride that way, stopping beside the two security guards holding them at bay.

"Y'all here to see Winter?" I ask the crowd.

A woman at the front of the crowd nods vigorously.

"Tell you what," I say. "If you'll leave your names and addresses with security, I'll personally make sure she sends you a signed photo. But we can't have everyone crowding up the halls. It's not safe for her or anyone else."

"Who are you?" someone demands.

"Her..." I almost say *man* and quickly stop myself. Shit. Is that what I am? We haven't put a label on it. It's fragile and new, but fuck. I am hers. I have been since word one. I will be until she orders me away. Even then, my heart will still belong to her. How can it not when she's the thing bringing it back to life? "Personal security."

"We just want to make sure she's all right," a young girl says from the back of the crowd.

"She appreciates that. But she's a little anxious about crowds right now. This"—I point at everyone—"isn't helping."

An uncomfortable murmur goes through the crowd.

"Is she ever going to perform again?" the same little girl asks.

"She is," I say. "But not until it's safe for her and for all of you for her to do that. The most important thing to her is making sure everyone is safe." I sweep my gaze over the group, my expression firm. "Crowding up a hospital corridor so the nurses can't even get through isn't safe. Let's give her a little space to visit with those who were hurt at the festival, all right? They need her right now."

"Okay, Mr. Bodyguard," the little girl says. "Can you please tell her that I'm glad she's okay? She doesn't have to send me a picture if she doesn't want. But I hope she keeps singing."

"Yeah, I'll tell her, sweetheart," I promise. "Leave your address with security for me. I'll make sure she sends you something, okay?"

"Okay! Bye!" she says, and then waves before skipping away.

One by one, everyone else in the crowd reluctantly follows after her, going back about their business. When a gap opens, I see Cash and Riley standing near the elevators with another couple I recognize, Cami and Bentley Reynolds. They played a show overseas a few years ago. Bentley wouldn't let anyone near his wife.

Riley's watching me with a big smile on her face.

"You handled that extremely well. I'm impressed," she says, walking toward me with her husband at her side. Cami and Bentley follow, Bentley's arm wrapped around Cami's shoulders.

"That was a walk in the park compared to some of the crowds we had to disperse overseas," I mutter. "No one was trying to fucking shoot me while I was talking."

Cash snorts.

Cami's eyes widen.

"Can you make sure we get a list of names and addresses for anyone who leaves them before we leave today?" I pause to ask one of the security guards.

"Fuck yeah," he says. "Thanks for getting them cleared out of here."

"You might want to block access to each unit as we enter," Riley suggests. "It'll keep crowds from forming and causing a traffic jam. There are only a few fans who haven't been discharged, so we shouldn't be here long."

"We'll do that," he says. "I'll pull some people from maintenance to help out."

"Thanks," Riley says, beaming at him. We walk a few feet away before she places a hand on my arm, halting me again. "How's she doing? I'm worried. She hasn't been answering her phone."

"Yeah, about that," I mutter, running a hand over my head. "I threw it out the window."

Riley blinks at me.

"Oh my," Cami whispers.

"Jesus Christ," Cash says, barking laughter.

Bentley just smirks.

"You threw it out the *window*?" Riley says. "Why in the world would you do that?"

"Didn't want anyone tracking her." It's only partly a lie, so I don't feel bad for telling it. I don't want anyone tracking her. And I don't fucking want any other men texting her either. If that makes me a possessive asshole, I'll own it. When it comes to her, I don't want to share her. I want to be the only man she's thinking about, the only one on her mind or in her space.

She snatched my heart right out of my chest and claimed it as her own. I intend to do the same. Until her heart belongs to me, I'm not giving anyone else a chance to slip beneath her defenses and take what I intend to possess. I don't know anything about making a girl like her fall in love, but I know war. The way I figure it, that saying *all's fair in love and war* is a saying for a reason. I'm not playing fair.

Cash sees right through me. He shakes his head, muttering *bullshit* through laughter.

Riley looks at him and then looks at me again. She opens her mouth and then closes it. "You know what? I'm not even going to yell at you right now for whatever weird caveman thing this is because I can tell by the look on your face that you aren't even sorry about it and I'd just be wasting my breath," she huffs. "But the next time you decide to toss her phone, do you think you might let her management team know?"

"I texted and told you that we were on the way here," I remind her.

"You didn't tell me that she had no phone!" Riley hisses, flinging her hands up. "If you had, I could have delivered the bad news when you were less likely to annoy me about it."

"What bad news?" I growl, instantly suspicious.

"She has one appearance we can't cancel." Riley jabs me in the chest with a pointy fingernail. "And don't even think about trying to make her skip it because she has to be there. It was her idea."

"What is it?" I demand.

"A fashion show."

I stare at her levelly.

"It's Gwen London's new line. Winter convinced half the curvy artists in Nashville to model the designs for her," she says. "We can't reschedule. It took a miracle to get everyone together on the same date in the first place."

"Jesus Christ," I mutter. "When is it?"

"Friday."

"That's three days from now."

"Aww. You can tell time. Good for you," Riley sasses.

I crack a smile, unable to help myself. "Are you always this savage?"

"Never," she lies, batting her lashes.

"Uh, that's a damn lie," Bentley says. "She's always savage."

Cash chuckles. "It means she likes you."

"Mind your business, Cash Jamison."

"Whatever you say, little goddess," he says, grinning at his wife like she hung the moon. I think as far as he's concerned, she did and no one can tell him any different. "Why don't you and Cami go check on Winter? We'll keep Ronan company out here in case anyone slips past security." He leans down, placing a hard kiss on her lips before I point Riley and Cami down the hallway.

"What do you know about Winter's parents?" I ask Cash as soon as they disappear into the room Winter went in a few minutes ago.

"They don't deserve her," he grunts. "Mom is a religious fanatic. Real Old Testament shit. Her dad goes along for the ride. They live about an hour from here. Why?"

I hesitate for a moment and then sigh. "I don't have any evidence, but I have a suspicion that her mother is the person we're looking for or is at least the brains behind the operation. The detectives are fairly certain whoever broke into her house is behind several of the letters she's received over the last year. They're far too familiar with her to be just a fan."

"Son of a bitch," Bentley growls.

"Fuck," Cash mutters, one dark brow flying upward. "How sure are you?"

"I don't have any proof if that's what you're asking," I murmur, keeping my voice pitched low so no one over-hears. The last thing Winter needs is for any of this to get out right now. "But I don't think whoever this is wants to kill her. I think they're trying to scare her into quitting. The letters and scriptures all heavily imply that Nashville is a sinful place and that she's surrounded by wickedness."

"Jesus Christ," Bentley says, shaking his head in disgust. "What kind of parent disowns their kid and then torments them like this?"

"One twisted by their own beliefs," Cash answers grimly before looking at me. "If you're right, it's going to break her fucking heart."

"Yeah, I know." Unfortunately, I don't think I'm wrong. Her mom is the one behind the attacks. I'd stake my life on it. The only thing I don't know is what the hell she's hoping to gain here. If she knows her daughter at all, she should know she isn't going to scare Winter into quitting. All she's going to do is get someone killed, potentially her own daughter.

Hell will freeze over before I allow it to go that far. I don't care if she is Winter's mom. If she endangers her life again, she'll answer to me. I've lost too goddamn much already. I'll be damned if I lose Winter too.

Chapter Seven

Winter

"Stop looking at me like that," I hiss at Riley, pressing my hands to my cheeks to hide the way they burn. She keeps grinning at me like she knows something I don't know. Every time she does it, Cami hides a smile behind her hand. I feel like a teenager with her first crush instead of a grown woman sitting in a private hospital waiting room with two of her best friends.

"I'm just looking at you," Riley says.

"No, you aren't," I grumble, pulling an oversized pair of sunglasses out of my pocket and plunking them down on my face.

Cami laughs quietly. "Stop teasing her, Riley. You're embarrassing her."

"Why did he throw your phone out the window?" Riley asks.

"He didn't want anyone to track it."

"He's in love with you," she says.

"What?" I yank the glasses off my face to gape at her. "Who? What? No, he isn't."

"Yeah, he is," she says.

"Is not," I mutter, my heart doing flips in my chest. "He's just doing his job."

"Oh, really?" She arches a brow, smirking at me. "Then why did he really throw your phone out the window?"

"He didn't want anyone to track it," I mumble again.

"Mmhmm," she hums, her smirk growing. "Who were you texting when he threw it out the window, Winter?"

"Memphis. Why does that...?" I trail off, my eyes widening. Is she trying to tell me that he threw my phone out because he was jealous? Oh my gosh! He did, didn't he? That's why he was so cranky about it. He didn't want me texting Memphis or anyone else. I stare at Riley in shock.

"He has it bad for you," she says.

"What am I going to do?" I whisper.

"Uh, him!" she says, laughing. "Preferably as often as possible."

"Riley!" Cami says.

"What? She has it just as bad as he does. It's written all over her face." Riley points at me. "She's practically glowing. She did not look this way two days ago."

"It's too fast," I blurt, standing up to pace around the small waiting room. I'm pretty sure it's where doctors bring families to deliver bad news. There are only half a dozen chairs and two small end tables. The art on the walls is meant to be soothing, but it's the same dull artwork found in most hospitals...the lifeless, sterile kind that serves only to remind you where you are and offers no comfort. "Isn't it too fast?"

It doesn't feel fast. I think I fell in love with him when he said he wanted to work for me because I need him. I fell again when he pulled me into his bed with him last night. I look at him and my heart aches to know what it feels like to belong to him. He cries out in pain and my heart does too. I'm in love with him. So damn in love with him.

"There is no such thing as too fast," Cami says gently. "The heart knows exactly how it feels. The head is what gets in the way and makes everything complicated."

"True story. I knew how I felt about Cash about two seconds after I met him, but I freaked out because I thought it was too fast and we weren't a good fit. I'm curvy and he's freaking hot." She rolls her eyes dramatically. "Our brains are stupid when it comes to love."

"Mine was so stupid," Cami agrees, her expression soft and rueful. Like me, Cami can be shy, only it's a lot worse for her. She's one of the sweetest people I've ever met.

"It was different for you two," I mumble, sinking down into a chair. I nudge my toe against a knot in the carpet.

"Things haven't been easy for him. He lost his whole team overseas. He's suffered so much." Tears well in my eyes at the thought of everything he's been through. Of everything he's still going through. "He still struggles so much. I think he feels guilty about what happened to his team. I don't... is it fair of me to ask him to give up what little peace he's found to live in my world?"

My world isn't peaceful. It's loud and cramped and busy. I spend half of my time surrounded by screaming fans or living on a tour bus. It's different cities every night with thousands of screaming fans or cameras shoved in my face. He's already sacrificed so much. How can I ask him to sacrifice what peace he's been able to carve out for himself to follow me around the world when I know how hard he's fought for what little peace he's found? It seems so selfish to even consider it.

He said I wasn't meant to be kept in a cage. But he wasn't made to suffer either. Is that what loving me will be like for him? A lifetime of suffering in silence just so we can be together?

"How do you know that's what you'd be asking him to do?" Riley asks.

"What do you mean?"

"I mean I see the way he looks at you," she says. "He doesn't look like a man who feels like he's giving up anything to be close to you. From where I'm sitting, he looks a whole lot like a man staring at salvation when he looks at you." She shrugs. "Seems to me that maybe the peace he's been looking for is sitting right here, worried about taking it away from him."

Cami nods her agreement. "Peace isn't a place, Winter. Sometimes, it's a person. That's what Bentley is for me. As nervous as I get about singing in crowds or putting myself out there, so long as he's beside me, I know I can do it."

I consider that for a long, silent moment. Maybe they're right. I don't know. All I know for sure is that I'm in love with Ronan and I don't want to give him up, not now and not when I'm safe. The thought alone makes my stomach cramp. Which means there's only one thing left to do.

Pull up my big girl panties and tell him how I feel.

"You're too quiet," he growls, cornering me in the kitchen as soon as we get home an hour later. His face is set in a hard, disapproving line as he backs me up against the counter, blocking me in with his arms on either side of me. "I don't like it, songbird."

"I'm just thinking," I murmur.

A growl rumbles in his chest, making me smile. He says so much without saying a word. I love that about him. I don't have to guess to know how he feels about any given subject. He makes his feelings clear with a well-timed grunt or growl or grumble or a disgruntled look. It shouldn't be nearly as endearing as it is, yet I love it.

"Thank you for taking me to the hospital today. It meant a lot to me."

His expression softens. "I'd do anything for you, Winter."

"Except let me text my band."

His gaze slides from mine, but not before I see the brief flare of guilt light his eyes. Riley was right. That is why he threw my phone out of the window.

"They're like my brothers, you know," I whisper and then grimace ruefully. "They even annoy me like brothers most of the time."

His gaze shifts back to mine. "Doesn't change the fact that I'm jealous as hell of anyone with a dick who makes you smile," he mutters. "Maybe it makes me an asshole, but I want to be the center of your world, songbird." He wraps his hand around my throat, tilting my face up to taste my lips. "I want to be the only man you're thinking about."

"You are," I whisper.

"Yeah?" He nips my bottom lip. "You thinking about me right now, Winter?"

"Yes."

"Are you thinking about what we did last night?"

"Y-yes."

"Good," he growls, running his tongue along my bottom lip. "Because I intend to do it again tonight, songbird. But

I'm not stopping this time. I'm taking what belongs to me."

"What belongs to you?" I manage to gasp. Lord, how does he manage to send my thoughts skittering away so quickly? All he has to do is touch me and I lose the ability to think straight. When he kisses me, I can't breathe. It's as if every cell in my body focuses on him and the little shocks of electricity zipping through my system, setting off fires all over the place.

"That delicious little cherry," he breathes against my lips.

I groan, my core clenching. "You know?"

"That I'm the only one who has ever had my cock near your cunt? Yeah, I know," he grunts before pulling me into a searing kiss that leaves my knees weak. "I can smell it all over you, songbird. I feel it when you touch me. You saved yourself for me, didn't you?"

"Yes," I whisper, trembling in his embrace. Growing up the way I did meant I didn't date. I was the only girl in school who never had a boyfriend or had even been kissed. When I started college, I spent all of my time focused on music. I didn't have time to focus on dating. And then I signed with Riley's team.

I've been asked out a lot in the last two years, but I've always said no. The men who asked—those like Logan Hayes who are known to sleep around—never interested me. And I never trusted anyone enough to let my guard down. In Nashville, it's hard to tell who is genuine and who is just playing the game. I didn't want to be a hot news item for someone. I didn't want to be a publicity stunt or a strategic move. I wanted something real with someone real. I wanted...Ronan.

I think I'd say yes to anything he asked. I wouldn't even hesitate.

"Good girl," he croons, his hand tight around my throat. His forest green eyes glitter with the hot stamp of possession. "You belong to me, songbird. This body belongs to me. That perfect little cunt belongs to me. I'm claiming it."

"Ronan," I moan, my core constricting. "Make me yours. Make love to me."

"Nah, songbird. Not yet," he breathes. "Not until I see those pouty lips wrapped around my cock. I've been thinking about it for days now."

As soon as he says it, I want it too.

I push against his shoulders, urging him back a step and then one more. He backs up just enough to give me a little room, a silent question in his eyes. I answer it when I drop to my knees right there on the kitchen floor.

"Fuck," he growls, heat flaring in his eyes. "You want it too, don't you?"

"Yes." I look up, locking eyes with him. "Teach me, Ronan."

He growls again, a rumbling, dangerous sound that vibrates in my soul as he reaches for his zipper. His eyes glitter with need, his chest rising and falling in a steady rhythm as he tugs his zipper down. I watch him through hooded lids, awed all over again at how powerful he is. He's a giant among men, a warrior in every sense of the word.

My breath wooshes from my lungs when he frees his erection. I saw it last night in the moonlight, but somehow I let myself forget how impressive it truly is. He's fiercely built, his erection jutting thick and proud from his body. Moisture beads the broad head as he wraps his fist around his shaft, working it up and down.

"Christ," he growls, staring down at me. "It's fucked up how much I like the sight of you on your knees eager to suck my cock, songbird."

"I like it too," I admit, swiping my tongue across my bottom lip as I lean forward, steadying myself with my palms against his powerful thighs. I don't feel small or overpowered by him. The way he trembles with desire makes me feel strong and powerful, confident in a way I've never been before. He's trembling because he wants me this badly. He's this hard because he's dying to feel my lips wrapped around him. I haven't even touched him yet, and I'm already unraveling him. "Teach me, Ronan. I've never done this before."

"Fuck," he groans, squeezing his cock. "Wrap your hand around my dick, songbird."

He curses when I obey his instruction, replacing his hand with mine. He's hot and hard in my hand, and so thick my fingers don't even meet around his shaft. I drag my hand up and down, exploring him. He pants, growling curses up at the ceiling.

I explore lower, stroking two fingers along his balls. They're tight and heavy.

"Goddamn," he growls, grasping my hair in his fist. He cranes my head back gently, locking eyes with mine. His are on fire, blazing hotter than the sun. "Don't do that again unless you want me fucking your pretty little throat."

"Do it," I whisper.

A string of curses rips from his lips. He loves it though. I see it in his eyes. The fire. The excitement. He loves that I'm eager and that I challenge him. It turns him on to know that I want him to do whatever he wants to me, that I'd let him do it.

"Dangerous woman," he mutters. "You're tempting a desperate man."

"Then take me, Ronan," I breathe, stroking his cock. "Own me. I want it."

He growls again, stepping toward me. "Wrap your lips around the head of my cock then, songbird. Let's see how perfect that hot little mouth feels."

I obediently lean forward, flicking my tongue out to touch it to the head of his cock. His taste hits my system like a wrecking ball. He's salty, masculine. I moan and wrap my lips around him, eager for more.

"Ah, goddamn," he groans, his hand tightening in my hair as I lick all around the head, gathering every little bead of moisture I can find. "You're going to ruin me, aren't you? I know you are. You sing like a fucking angel and suck cock like you were born to do it."

I pull him deeper into my mouth, moaning around his length.

He growls, his hips moving restlessly, as if he wants to thrust but is trying to hold himself back. I wrap my hands around his thighs and tug, silently pleading with him to take what he wants. I want him to control this. I want him to take his pleasure from me. There's something sexy about the thought.

"You want this, songbird?" he asks, thrusting gently.

I moan, bobbing my head.

"Fuck," he groans, holding my hair in one fist as he pulls back slightly and then thrusts forward again. His erection slides deeper, stretching my mouth wide. I moan around him, urging him on. His eyes narrow to half-mast, glittering with lust.

"Christ, you look good with my dick in your mouth, Winter." He pumps his hips again, taking my mouth in shallow, steady thrusts. "Hollow your cheeks. Suck hard."

I try to obey, but he picks up the pace, gliding in and out of my mouth faster. The head of his cock touches the back of my throat and I gag around him, choking on him.

"Fuck," he groans, pulling back before he thrusts forward again. "I feel your throat closing around me." He does it again and then again, cursing every time I choke on him.

His eyes blaze hotter and then hotter still, until staring at him feels like staring into the face of the sun. He loves it.

So do I. I lick and suck, reveling in the feel of him in my mouth. In the sounds he makes. In the way he trembles every time he touches the back of my throat. I work my hand up and down what doesn't fit in my mouth, trying to touch everywhere at once. And then his comment from earlier pops into my head. I slip my hand further back, fondling his balls again.

"Fuck!" he roars, his hand tightening in my hair. He holds my head still. "I warned you songbird. You didn't listen." He pushes forward, thrusting to the back of my throat. "Swallow."

I try, but only manage to choke on him again.

He eases off to let me breathe. "Again," he growls. "Swallow around me this time. Let me have what I want." He thrusts forward again, fierce, relentless. I gag on him again and he immediately backs off, his eyes glittering with lust. When he thrusts forward the third time, I manage to swallow at just the right time. He slips down my throat.

My eyes widen in shock.

His flare with triumph.

He rocks his hips, thrusting until I can't breathe and my eyes water, and then he backs off slightly. "Take a breath," he orders, his voice little more than a dark growl. "I'm going to fuck your perfect little throat."

Oh my god.

I suck in a breath, quivering in want.

He growls and lets go, rocking his hips into me until his balls nearly touch my chin. He holds himself there for a moment, pulsing his hips, cursing. I sob, clawing at his thighs, so turned on it physically hurts. He eases back for me to breathe and then thrusts forward again.

"Goddamn, songbird," he groans. "You feel so fucking good. Christ, I could do this to you all day." He pulses his hips again. "Look at how pretty you look with tears running down your face and my cock down your throat. Jesus" He runs his thumbs gently over my cheeks, his expression reverent and adoring. "So beautiful."

I moan around him.

He curses again and then pulls back, slipping from my lips. Before I can protest, I'm in his arms and he's storming toward the bedroom like the hounds of hell nip at his heels. I suck in a deep breath and then another, shaking in need. I think I'm coming apart at the seams.

"Ronan," I whimper, so turned on it's a little terrifying.

"I know," he growls. "I've got you."

As soon as we cross the threshold, he tosses me toward the bed. I bounce when I land. Before I even settle, he's on top of me, wrestling me to my back. His mouth comes down on mine in a punishing kiss. He devours my mouth, claiming it like he intends to possess it.

"It's my turn to make you feel good, songbird," he breathes, running his hands all over my body. He lifts me up, quickly stripping me out of my shirt and bra. His palms glide across my nipples, teasing the hard peaks. "I'm going to make you scream, pretty baby."

"Ronan," I plead.

He leans down, capturing my nipple in his mouth.

I claw at his shoulders, crying out in bliss as his teeth close around it.

He does the same thing to the other before kissing a hot trail down my stomach.

My clit pulses when he shoves his face between my legs and smells me.

"Fuck," he groans, drawing the word out. "Peaches and pussy might be my new favorite scent, Winter."

"Ronan!" I cry, shocked when he opens his mouth over my center and just...latches on. He doesn't warn me or anything. He just goes for it, licking me right through my leggings and panties.

He grunts, pressing against my clit with his mouth.

My hips arch off the bed, a sharp cry ringing out around us. He doesn't even bother removing my leggings and panties. He just tears the crotch out of them to get to me.

"Oh, fuck yeah," he growls, spreading my legs wide. "Look how sweet it is. I bet it's going to gush in my mouth, isn't it? Fuck. I *know* it is." I don't think he's talking to me. I think he's talking to himself, the words in his mind slipping out as if he can't control them. He leans forward, licking me from top to bottom.

"Ronan!" I shout, sobbing as a blast of pleasure rips through me.

He drags me closer to his mouth, snarling. I get lost then, the world spiraling away as he attacks me like a man brought to the brink. I cling to the blankets for dear life, sobbing for mercy as he eats me as if he's never tasted anything sweeter. Pleasure piles on pleasure, building to a flashpoint so intense I know it's going to break me when I erupt.

He thrusts his tongue into my hole, fucking me with it before he replaces it with two fingers and attacks my clit with that wicked tongue. I sob his name, shouting it into the room until it echoes and bounces back to us. His curses bounce back too, creating a harmony that's sexier than any song I've ever heard.

I lose my grip on reality entirely when he wraps his lips around my tongue and curls his fingers up at the same time, stroking against my g-spot. Fireworks erupt behind my eyelids, sending me catapulting over the edge into a fiery orgasm. It's the best thing I've ever felt.

Until he prowls up my body, pressing his cock to my opening.

"I can't wait," he growls, grinding against my clit. "I need in you, songbird."

"Yes, yes," I chant, still caught in the throes of my orgasm, riding the high. "Now, Ronan. Get in me now."

He groans my name, his lips seeking mine as he lines up at my entrance. I taste myself on his lips as he pushes forward. If there's any pain as he fills me, it's fleeting. All I feel is full. So damn full. He's everywhere, sheltering me in his strong embrace, kissing me, grinding against my clit. I feel him in my soul, nestling into place where he belongs.

"Ronan, I love you," I whisper against his lips as his hips settle against mine.

He falls still, his forest eyes flashing to mine.

"I love you," I whisper again.

"Jesus," he breathes. He presses his forehead to mine, a tremor moving through his big body. "I love you, songbird. Since the minute I met you."

"Then love me."

He touches his lips to mine again and then begins to move. He's so powerful, like a storm raging as he pulls back and then thrusts forward, filling me again and again. We kiss and touch as he teaches me what it means to love like this. What it means to be complete. I sob against his lips, overwhelmed by how good he feels. By how deep he is. By how excruciatingly perfect this moment feels, as if the rest of the world exists far outside of this moment.

"Goddamn, songbird," he rasps in my ear. "I'm never going to be able to stop now that I know how fucking perfect you feel. You've already got my dick addicted to you."

"Me too," I cry, raking my nails down his back as I try to pull him closer. "Me too."

"You gotta come for me," he groans, reaching between us to stroke my clit.

I sob his name, the coil in my stomach tightening.

"That's it, baby," he croons. "Come all over me."

I try to tell him that I'm going to, but all I manage to do is groan his name before he presses his thumb to my clit. I shatter into a thousand pieces, scattering to the winds.

He roars, pounding into me without rhythm as he follows me over the edge.

I cling to his shoulders, riding out the waves as he groans my name again and again, filling me so full he spills out, running down my thighs.

We collapse together, a tangle of arms and legs and panted breaths.

"I'm keeping you, songbird," he breathes in my ear, holding me close.

"Okay," I whisper back.

Chapter Eight

Ronan

"You didn't have nightmares last night, " Winter says, watching me intently from her chair in the gym.

"I know." I finish my set and replace the weight on the bench before prowling across the room toward her. "A curvy little songbird crawled into my bed and swore to help me fight them a few nights ago. She's a helluva soldier."

"Is she?" she whispers, tilting her head back for me to kiss her.

I do, hard and deep.

My nightmares aren't cured. I have no illusions about that. PTSD doesn't go away just because we want it to. Falling in love doesn't magically erase trauma. But having her pressed up against me when I sleep helps more than anything else ever has. She roots me to reality better than anything ever has. It's hard to get lost in memories of the past when the most important part of my future is in my arms, counting on me to help keep her safe.

In the two days since I made her mine, we've spent a lot of time in bed together. I can't keep my damn hands to myself. All she has to do is look at me, and I want to fuck her again. We've been in our own bubble.

But it can't last forever. Riley and Cash will be here in a couple of hours to go over the game plan for the fashion show tomorrow. And then we have the fashion show to-morrow. I'm seriously fucking worried it's going to bring her mom out of hiding. Or prompt some other psycho to try the same bullshit.

Anderson is dragging his feet about questioning her mom. He doesn't want to tip her off that we suspect her. I'm not thrilled with this plan. It means they intend to let her try something else before they make a move. She's already demonstrated that she's willing to hurt people.

If anything happens to Winter, I won't survive. I'm not sure I'll want to survive it. I survived losing everything once. I've been haunted for two fucking years because I couldn't get to my team fast enough to save them. I'm even haunted by the shit I did and the motherfuckers I killed in the mountains to stay alive—and they deserved it. But I don't know how to survive being haunted by Winter. Seeing her everywhere but being unable to touch her. Hearing an echo of her but never that beautiful voice. How do you live without your heart when it's the only thing that keeps you going?

Loving her brought me back to life. I have a purpose again. My world has meaning again. Every inch of it is painted with her. I can't lose her. God only knows what I'll do if anything happens to her.

"I love you," she whispers against my lips.

I breathe those words into my lungs, letting them flow through my veins. Love isn't strong enough to describe how I feel about this songbird. It doesn't even come close to explaining the way my heart beats for her. I would die for her without hesitation.

"Come on," I murmur, pulling her to her feet. "You can show me how much while you're playing with yourself in the shower."

"Ronan," she groans.

"Don't groan at me, baby," I growl, tapping her on the ass to get her moving. "We both know what I'll find if I put my hands in your panties right now. You come to the gym because watching me work out makes you horny for my cock."

We both know it's true. I offered to show her how the treadmill worked yesterday when she showed up and she looked at me like I'd just sprouted two heads and horns, then politely told me where I could stick my treadmill. Let me just say, it won't fit where she suggested.

"Fine," she huffs, shooting me a look over her shoulder. "But do I get to watch you too?"

"No." I drag her up against me, pressing my lips to her ear. "Because as soon as you make yourself come, I'm going to bend you over and fuck you from behind while I play with your other little hole."

She moans, melting into me.

I press a kiss to her throat, fighting the urge to press her up against the wall and have my way with her here and now. Jesus. She'll be pregnant in a matter of days at the rate we're going. Hell, if she isn't already. I hope like hell she is. I want her round with my kid so the whole world knows she's mine and they don't stand a chance. I won't give her up now. Not even hell itself could drag me away from this woman.

My cell vibrates in my pocket.

"Ignore it," Winter whispers, shifting her ass against my cock.

For a split second, I consider doing precisely that and then sigh. "It could be important, songbird. Let me take care of it, and then you can show me how dirty you can be for me."

She groans in protest, pressing her face against my throat.

I pull my phone out of my pocket, cursing when I see Riley's name on the display. If she's calling, there's no way it's anything I want to hear. She's basically a terrorist in stilettos. But she has Winter's best interests at heart and is firmly in her corner.

"Good morning, Riley," I say, putting the phone to my ear.

"You're in way too good of a mood," she complains. "I liked you better when you were cranky and didn't talk. You didn't annoy me nearly as much then."

Winter hears her and giggles.

"Rough morning?" I ask, smiling despite myself. I like Riley. She's feisty, but she hides a heart of gold underneath all that sass and sarcasm. No one who knows her has ever had a bad word to say about her. She inherited her company young and has used it to help change the face of country music. She knows her shit and takes no shit.

"I'll tell you about it when we get there," she says. "We're on the way. Detective Anderson is coming too." She pauses. I can feel the tension radiating down the line. "It's not good news, Ronan."

Fuck. I knew it was coming sooner or later, but I really fucking hoped it'd be later. Preferably after the fashion show tomorrow. I guess our luck has run out though.

"How far out are you?" I sigh.

"Fifteen minutes."

"We'll be ready."

Ty Anderson, Cash, and Riley pull into the driveway eighteen minutes later. Like usual, Cash is dressed down—a black t-shirt and jeans. Riley is dressed to kill. And Ty is in a suit, his gun in a shoulder holster. They look somber as they approach the front door.

Riley pulls Winter in for a hug, whispering something in her ear. Winter whispers something back, and then they hug again. Cash taps her on the nose, grinning at her. She gives him a tiny smile, anxiety written all over her face.

"Miss Pyke," Anderson says, in formal cop mode.

"Detective Anderson, please come in." She holds the door open wide for him, inviting him into my house. He steps through the door, taking a quick glance around before his gaze comes to me. "Captain Gallagher?"

"Retired," I mutter.

He jerks his chin in a nod. "Good to finally put a face to the voice."

"You too." He's exactly what I expected—mid-thirties, broad shoulders, clean-cut. His demeanor screams hard-ass cop.

"What's going on?" Winter asks, not wasting time.

I pull her into me, wrapping an arm around her waist.

Anderson's gaze flickers between the two of us—*yeah, motherfucker, she's mine*—before he focuses on her again, not commenting on the two of us. Smart of him. "Mrs. Jamison received another letter addressed to you last night, Miss Pyke," he says calmly. "We have reason to believe it was from the individual responsible for what happened at the festival."

The color drains from Winter's face.

"Fuck," I growl, tugging her closer to me.

"W-what does it say?" she whispers.

Riley and Cash share a look.

"I don't think you should read it," Riley says gently. "It's just the ravings of a crazy person, Winter. It doesn't mean anything."

"What does it say?" she asks again, her voice stronger this time.

Riley looks at me.

I hesitate for a brief second and then reluctantly nod. I don't want her to read it either, but she has a right to know. It's her life, her choice. No one else gets to decide for her what she is or isn't strong enough to handle. No one gets to decide what she has a right to know about the things that impact her life. Besides, there may be something in it to help us figure out who the fuck sent it. She's the only one who can tell us if she recognizes anything in it.

Riley sighs and motions for Detective Anderson.

"This is a copy," he says, reaching into his breast pocket. "I've already sent the original off for testing. Hopefully, we can pull fingerprints or some sort of DNA since no one handled it. Mrs. Jamison called us as soon as she recognized the envelope." He passes the letter to Winter who accepts it with shaking hands.

I pull her in front of me, wrapping my arms around her waist so we can read it together. So I can hold onto her while she reads. I don't want her reading it alone. Fuck that. She doesn't do anything alone anymore.

How long will the wicked be jubilant when they're paying for their sins, Winter?
Return to righteousness or be destroyed with them.
Repent or dwell in the silence of death.
The pit has been dug.

"Jesus Christ," I growl, snatching the letter out of her hands when she makes a strangled noise. I crumple it, tossing it toward Cash as I spin her around to face me. "It's bullshit, songbird. Do you hear me? It's bullshit."

"It's a psalm," she whispers, her expression wan. "Psalm 94."

"You know it?" Anderson asks.

"I know it," she mumbles. "But whoever wrote this twisted it all up. They made it threatening and ominous. That's not what the psalm is supposed to be. It's a reminder that God knows all, and He alone is responsible for judging. It's supposed to bring comfort, not be used to condemn." She lifts her eyes to me, her expression worried. "I think...I think I know who wrote this."

"Who, songbird? Was it your mom?"

"My mom?" She blinks wide eyes at me. "No, of course not. I think it was her pastor, though. Brother Gibbs used to twist scripture like this all the time. He's...misguided," she says carefully. "He tries to make God in his image. Women in his church aren't allowed to hold jobs. They aren't allowed to do a lot of things. You marry within the church, and you never really leave. You're just kind of stuck."

"Jesus Christ," I growl. "That's not a church, songbird. It's a cult."

"Yeah," she whispers sadly. "I guess it is. I don't know why he hates me so much. Maybe he's angry that I got out and others may follow? I don't know. But I think it's him." She shivers. "This letter feels like him. I don't think he's very well. Mentally, I mean."

"How did you get out?" Anderson asks.

"My high school counselor." She smiles wistfully. "She convinced me to apply for college and helped me with scholarship applications. When my dad realized they weren't going to have to pay for anything, he figured there wasn't any harm in letting me attend since I wanted to go so badly. Since it was a Christian school, it seemed harmless enough to him. I didn't tell them that I was playing shows around town until I'd signed a contract with Riley. They barely speak to me now."

The tremor in her voice kills me. Fuck her parents. Fuck her former pastor. She always deserved better. There isn't a wicked bone in her body. She may be in Nashville, singing in front of sold out crowds, but she's got better odds of getting into heaven than anyone else I know. She certainly has betters odds than whoever the fuck thinks they have a right to play God and judge and condemn her for following her heart.

"Until testing comes back on the letter and envelope, we'll put a car on him," Anderson says, looking from her to me. "See if we can't find some strong evidence that he's the one behind this. Just keep her out of sight until then."

"Yeah, about that," I mutter. "She has a fashion show to attend tomorrow."

"Cancel it," he says. "The last place she needs to be is a fashion show."

"No."

He looks at her.

"I've done everything you've asked me to do," she says, her voice firm. "I've stayed out of sight. I hired a bodyguard. I've cooperated. I've literally stopped living my life to give you guys time to catch the person responsible. But people are counting on me to be there tomorrow. I'm going."

"We've hired extra security," Riley says. "We'll have a dozen armed guards inside the venue, and a dozen more outside. Everyone who comes in will pass through metal detectors. We've done everything possible to ensure that everyone will be safe tomorrow. If you want to send officers to make it even safer, feel free."

Anderson grinds his teeth together, clearly not pleased that two tiny little women are gainsaying him. But he knows when he's outnumbered. "Fine," he growls, backing down. "But if anything happens, you get to stand in front of the media at the press conference and answer their questions."

"Fine," Riley snaps while Cash glowers at him. "They'd probably prefer to hear from me anyway. At least I actually answer questions."

Anderson leaves before Riley and Cash. I think Riley pissed him off. Sucks for him because she's right. People would rather hear from her than him. She has charisma and charm. He's about as charming as a bear coming out of hibernation.

I leave Winter inside to walk Riley and Cash to Cash's truck after we devise a plan for tomorrow. It's not much of one. Winter and I will get there half an hour before she's set to walk the runway. She'll do her thing, and then we'll duck out the back. By the time the show ends, we'll be long gone. Hopefully, it'll keep the emphasis on Gwen and her design as intended and help keep Winter out of the spotlight as much as possible.

I'd much rather not go at all, but I'm not going to ask her to cancel. This matters to her. Her friends matter to her. Right now, she needs them. She needs to remember that she has people in her corner and that she carved out an incredible life for herself when she walked away from her family and the way she was raised. I think she could use that reminder now more than ever.

That fucking letter shook her up, exactly as it was meant to do. I can see it in her eyes. She's scared, more so for the people around her, I think, than she is for herself. This bastard has already shot her guitarist and caused a stampede at her show, injuring two dozen of her fans. What else is he capable of doing? Who else might he hurt to get to her? To unravel her and make her question the choices she's made?

I want to find him and rip him limb from fucking limb for putting her through this. A man of God doesn't threaten his flock. He doesn't terrorize or torment them. A man of God doesn't appoint himself as judge, jury, and executioner. She's done nothing to deserve condemnation.

By the time I make it back inside, Winter is on the couch, plucking out a melancholy tune on her guitar. Her cat is curled up on the chaise across from her, sleeping. I think that's the only thing the cat does...sleep and eat. Actually, I take that back. She blows up the litter box too. Worse than

Keller used to blow up the bathrooms after eating chili. I need a Hazmat suit just to scoop the damn box.

"Working on a new song?" I ask, leaning back against the wall to watch her.

"Finishing one," she says, reaching for the pen and notepad beside her. She jots something in it, frowns, scratches it out, and then jots something else. After a moment, she plucks a few more strings, humming quietly.

"Sing it for me, songbird."

She looks up at me.

"I want to hear it."

A pretty blush steals across her face. "I haven't even practiced it yet."

"I don't care."

She takes a deep breath and then nods, adjusting her guitar on her lap. She strums a few chords, humming quietly, and then she starts to sing.

Drank too much again last night.
Watched it all just pass me by
Doing anything and everything just to get you off my mind.
I don't think it's working now.
Because I still can't take a breath.

I'm going down.
Knees on the concrete
Head in my hands.

Can you hear me?
I'm going down.

Thought I could outlast you.
That I could watch you walk away.
I was crazy for thinking it.
Crazy for believing I didn't need you to survive.
So I drank too much again last night
Trying to keep you off my mind.

But I'm going down.
Knees on the concrete
Head in my hands.
Can you hear me?
I'm going down.

I need you, baby.
Please.
I need you.

Her voice fades on the last line. She strums another few chords and then the guitar falls silent. I stare at her for a long moment, my heart pounding against my ribcage like a war drum. My dick pressed so firmly against my zipper I feel the teeth of it digging into my shaft.

"When did you start writing it?" I ask.

"When I realized I was falling in love with you," she whispers, lifting her gaze to mine. There's so much vulnerability in her eyes, so much honesty it wrecks me. "I thought if I pretended it wasn't happening, I could make it stop. But then I heard you crying out in your sleep and realized that I was going down no matter what." She swallows hard. "I don't regret it, Ronan."

"Fuck," I growl, stomping across the room toward her with my heart in my throat. I take her guitar from her, propping it carefully against the couch before I pull her into my arms. "I don't regret it either, songbird. Loving you is the best goddamn thing that's ever happened to me."

"Then love me right now," she pleads. "Make me forget all about that letter and how cold I feel. Bring me back to life, Ronan. Please."

"You don't even have to ask," I whisper, scooping her up into my arms to carry her to our bedroom. "You never have to ask me to love you. The answer is always yes."

Chapter Nine

Winter

Ronan carries me into the bedroom, kicking the door closed behind us to shut out the world. I expect him to put me down, but he doesn't. He carries me straight to the bed, laying me out in the center of it. I stare up at him, awed at how strong he is. At how strong he makes me feel.

Reading that letter made me feel so small and powerless, as if pieces of my identity and soul were being slowly chipped away. But the way he looks at me molds them back into place, reshaping me into something stronger, more beautiful. I'm not the little girl who grew up in a twisted church with parents who are ashamed of her. I'm not a country musician who has to be on all the time and is stretched thin. I'm just Winter, and that's enough.

"You're so fucking beautiful," he whispers, leaning down to press a reverent kiss to my lips. "Every time I look at you, I wonder how I got so fucking lucky."

"I think the same thing," I admit. "I get to walk with giants when I'm with you."

"And I get to love a legend." A ghost of a smile dances at his lips as he brushes my hair back from my face. His lips meet mine again, soft and sweet.

"Lucky you," I whisper against his lips.

His lips grow more insistent against mine, as if kissing me ignites a fire within him. I cling to him, kissing him back just as passionately, just as hungrily. My body trembles as he strips me naked, worshipping me with his lips and hands. He leaves no part of me untouched as my clothes drop to the floor.

His follow. I kiss every scar I unveil and trace every tattoo, leaving him trembling too.

"What was under these that you had to hide?" I ask, running my fingers over the black ones across his forearms.

"Ranger tattoos," he murmurs. "I couldn't look at them every day after what happened but it didn't feel right to have them removed, either."

I bring his arms to my mouth, pressing my lips to each one. "They don't blame you," I whisper.

"I know." He swallows, pulling me in for a kiss. "For the first time in two years, I actually believe that. You're teaching me that, songbird."

I press my lips to his again, running my hands down his abdomen, marveling at his strength and the vulnerability it hides. He's so many things, each of them beautiful.

By the time we're naked, I'm a ball of sensation, overwhelmed by how badly I need him. Nothing else matters. Nothing else exists. How can it when he's the only thing I see?

"Look at me, songbird," he says, slipping between my legs.

I glance down at him, crying out when I see the devotion blazing in his eyes. There's so much of it. God, the way this man loves me. It's written right there for the whole world to see and it's beautiful.

"You're so fucking perfect." He holds my gaze as he eats me, keeping me caught in a net of desire, tangled completely in him. I moan and shake beneath him, lost in bliss. It doesn't take him long to send me catapulting over the edge into heaven. With his eyes on me, everything feels a thousand times more intense, as if he's staring directly into my soul.

"I love you," he murmurs, hitching my leg up over his hip as I float back down to earth.

"Love you," I moan.

He thrusts forward, filling me. We cry out together, writhing in ecstasy. He makes love to me slowly, gently, slipping almost all the way out before pushing forward again. He keeps his eyes locked on mine the entire time, keeping me caught up in him and what he's doing to me. In the devotion in his gaze and the safety I find there.

I run my hands all over him, trying to touch him everywhere at the same time. His body is fascinating to me. So hard and strong, yet he's so much more than that. He's a little bit broken and battered and bruised, but so damn beautiful, inside and out. There is no one else in the world like him.

Sweet words spill from his lips, whispered into the room in a searing litany. He tells me exactly how he feels, holding nothing back. He loves me. I'm beautiful. Perfect. I belong to him.

"I love you," I whisper, tears slipping down my cheeks as he puts me back together and ruins me at the same time. I moan and twist and arch beneath him, racing toward the peak.

We tumble over the edge together, crying out as one. I fall into him, fall deeper for him.

"Forever, songbird," he breathes.

"I'll be fine," I tell Ronan for the fifth time since we arrived at the warehouse where we're doing Gwen's show. There are people everywhere, but it's organized chaos. "It's just a quick walk down the runway, and then we get to go back home."

"I like that you're calling my place home."

"It feels like home," I admit.

He grins at me, his eyes lighting up. "That's because you're in it, songbird. You make it feel that way." He presses his lips to my temple. "Go get ready to do your walk. I'll be right out here. If you need me, all you have to do is scream my name."

"It's a dressing room," I remind him. "Not much happens in here aside from a bunch of girls gossiping and drinking wine while we get pretty. I'll be fine."

"You're already beautiful."

I lean up on my toes, pressing my lips to his cheek. "I love you for thinking that, but there's no way I'm going out there looking like this, soldier." I look exactly like I was up all night making love. There are bags under my eyes, and I've got a hickey on my collarbone. I don't regret a single minute of it. I'd do it all again in a heartbeat.

"You mean ex-soldier," he growls, palming my ass. "Go get ready, songbird."

"Okay. I love you."

"I love you." He runs his finger down the center of my face, smiling at me.

I drag myself away from him, slipping inside the dressing room.

"Finally!" Gwen cries, rushing forward to grab my arm. "I didn't think you two were ever going to quit making out. Good grief. He's F-I-N-E fine, girl."

"I know, right?" I look at her with big eyes.

She cracks up, pulling me into a tight hug. "I've missed you so much!"

"I missed you too."

"I want all the details," she says, dragging me toward a makeup table where her best friend and Cyrus's sister, Jessa, is sitting, her makeup already fully done. She looks amazing. "Don't you dare leave anything out. I haven't had any good gossip in months."

"His name is Ronan Gallagher," I say, plopping down next to Jessa. "He's my bodyguard. And I'm madly in love with him."

"Uh, clearly!" Gwen cries, shoving a glass of wine into my hand. "You're glowing."

"You are glowing," Jessa agrees, smiling at me.

Gwen prods at the hickey on my neck. "We're going to have to cover that up."

I squeak, slapping a hand over it.

"Girl, please," she says, laughing. "Cyrus is forever leaving them on me."

"Jax does too," Jessa says, rolling her eyes. "I don't know what it is about our military men, but they all seem to share the same caveman tendencies, don't they?"

"Thank you, Uncle Sam," Gwen says.

Jessa raises her glass in a toast, making me giggle.

"You know Ronan was in the military?" I ask, sipping my wine.

"He has that look," Jessa says. "It's the eyes."

Gwen nods. "And the walk. You can always tell by the walk."

"He was a Ranger. He retired last year."

"We should get him together with Jax and Cyrus," Jessa says.

"He'd probably like that," I say quietly. "Um, his whole team was killed overseas two years ago. He was the only survivor. It's been tough for him."

"Damn," Gwen whispers, her expression falling. "We should definitely get them together then. Cyrus struggles with PTSD too. It'll be good for him to have someone to talk to who knows what it's like."

"I didn't know that," I murmur.

"It's not as bad for him now," she says. "But when he first got back a few years ago, it was really tough. We almost didn't make it because of everything he was going through."

I squeeze her arm, grateful they made it. She and Cyrus belong together.

"Speaking of Cyrus," she says, popping back up to her feet. "I better go make sure he's got everything under control out there."

"Oh, I'll go too," Jessa says. "I want to see my baby."

"The makeup artist should be back from her break in like five minutes," Gwen says. "You're the last one. So just hang out and wait. She'll get you taken care of when she gets in here, and then we'll get you dressed. You're walking second so we can get you out of here."

"Thank you."

"Thank *you*," she says, beaming at me. "You're the one who convinced everyone to help me make this thing happen today. I owe you for life."

"You don't owe me anything."

She blows me a kiss and then she and Jessa head out of the room. I sit back in the makeup chair and close my eyes, smiling. As much as I've enjoyed my bubble with Ronan, it feels good to be doing something normal today.

A few seconds later, the outside door opens.

I pop my eyes open to greet the makeup artist.

"M-mom?" I whisper, staring in shock at the woman standing not even five feet from me.

"Hello, dear," she says as if it hasn't been two years since we last saw each other.

"What are you doing here?"

"Why, I came to get you, of course."

My heart slams against my ribcage, the first inkling of fear rushing through me.

Chapter Ten

Ronan

I pace outside the dressing room, restless and uneasy as fuck. It's too crowded here. Too loud. I don't know if it's the PTSD talking, my worry for Winter, or if it's actually instinct telling me something is wrong, but my skin crawls. My chest feels tight. I want to burst through the fucking door, yank Winter out of there, and tell her that we're leaving. But this is important to her.

I can't drag her away just because I can't handle sharing her. Christ. Is that what this is about? I'm crawling out of my skin because I don't want to share her? Because I'm a jealous, possessive asshole who wants her all to myself?

No. I spent two decades in the military. Most of that time was in the Rangers, working recon. They sent us into every death trap on this planet. We slipped in and moved undetected. Until our last mission, we were virtual ghosts. No one saw us. No one heard us. We moved through occupied territory on damn near every continent behind enemy lines, and never got caught because we trusted our instincts. They never failed us. Even on the last mission, mine didn't fail me.

I knew something was wrong. Something didn't feel right. Something was *off*. It was the entire reason I stayed behind trying to get a signal on the goddamn radio while the team went ahead. We needed to establish contact because every single one of us felt the same bad energy. I never managed to raise our base. We were too deep into the fucking mountains for that. All I managed to do was overhear a transmission never intended for us. The one that confirmed everything we'd been feeling for two damn days. Something *was* off.

We weren't moving in silence this time, unseen and unheard. We were being stalked through the mountains, hunted like prey. I was too late to save my team. Despite everything, I couldn't get there fast enough to warn them that they were walking into the middle of a trap laid just for us. I watched as the village exploded, killing every single one of them. By the time I got there, there was nothing I could do for any of them.

I won't let that be Winter. My instincts aren't screaming at me because I don't want to share her. They aren't screaming at me because I'm still fucked up from what happened. They're screaming at me because I've been down this road. I know where it leads. Something is off.

"Hey." I grab the arm of the first woman who passes, a petite pregnant woman with jet-black hair and corn-flower-blue eyes. Riley introduced her earlier, but for a long moment, I can't remember her name. And then it hits me. Addison Devine. Her name is Addison Devine. "Can you go in and check on Winter for me?"

"Sure," she says, giving me a tiny, hesitant smile. "Is everything okay?"

"No," I growl. "I don't think so."

Her eyes widen. To her credit, she doesn't ask anything else. She jumps into action, scurrying into the dressing room without another word. I pace two steps to the right and then half a step to the left before she reappears.

"She isn't in there," she says.

"What?"

"She isn't in there."

"Fuck!" I roar. "Go find Riley. Tell her to get Anderson here now."

Addison bobs her head, but I'm already ducking past her into the dressing room, my heart pounding against my ribcage. Terror claws through me, threatening to drag me to my knees in the middle of the floor. I fight it, racing toward the only other exit in the room.

I burst through the door, running right into the security guard stationed outside.

"Where the fuck is she?" I snarl, grabbing him by the collar.

"W-who?"

"Winter!"

"She left with her mom."

Her mom. Ah, Jesus Christ. Her mom has her.

Sometimes, being right is a real bitch. This is going to break her heart.

"Which way did they go?" I growl, releasing his collar.

"They just went toward the overflow parking lot," he says.

I pull my gun.

"Jesus Christ," he breathes, reaching for his.

"Try to shoot me and you'll live long enough to regret it," I snap. "Her mom is the one who tried to shoot her, you fucking moron."

The color slides from his face. "What?"

"Send everyone available to the parking lot to help look for her."

"If I lose my job for this..."

"If you lose your job, it'll be for letting her fucking mom in the goddamn building without sending her through the front," I growl. "It won't be for sending me back up to protect her." I turn and run toward the overflow parking lot, not waiting around to see if he gets on the radio to get back up or not. I don't have time to waste.

I pray as I run, pleading with God to let me get there in time. I haven't prayed in years. Fuck, I'm not sure I even believe in God anymore. But I beg him to hear me now, to help me find her before her mother manages to get her out of here and we lose her trail.

I can't lose her. I won't lose her.

"Winter!" I shout, scanning the crowded lot for her "Where are you, songbird?"

A muffled cry from the back of the lot bounces back from the sky.

"Winter!" I roar, charging that way.

I dodge around a pickup truck and my girl comes into view. A lady in her fifties or early sixties clutches her arm in a vise-grip, practically dragging her toward a white SUV a few car lengths ahead.

"Stop," I growl, aiming my weapon at the woman's back. "I'll shoot you where you fucking stand."

She spins around, dragging Winter around with her. I can tell just by looking that they're related. They share the same amber eyes. Though Winter's blaze with love as they land on me. Her mother's burn with madness.

"I'm taking my daughter home," she says.

"You aren't taking my future wife anywhere," I disagree, my voice dangerously soft. "You lost any claim you had on her when you turned your back on her two years ago. She isn't yours anymore. She never will be again."

"She doesn't belong in this God-forsaken city!"

"She doesn't belong in your God-forsaken excuse of a home either," I roar. "What kind of parent spends a year sending their child sick, twisted letters threatening her life and those of the people she loves? What kind of parent fires a fucking weapon at her on a stage? Injures innocent people?"

Her mother's face blanches. "You think I had something to do with that? It's the reason I'm taking her home!" she cries. "I've watched from afar for two years, letting her live her life. But I draw the line at letting music destroy her. I won't watch her die for it!"

Fuck me. She's telling the truth. It wasn't her.

"Brother Gibbs," Winter whispers. "It was Brother Gibbs."

"He wouldn't do that," her mom protests weakly.

"Yes, he would," Winter disagrees. "You know he would, Mama. You may pretend you don't see what kind of man he is, but we both know you do. He isn't a good man. He never has been, and you know it."

Her mom's confidence wavers.

"He isn't a man of God," Winter says, her voice soft. "You just don't want to admit it because you don't want to admit that you've been misled all these years. But you have been misled. He uses you and everyone else in the congregation for his own purposes. He always has. He manipulates and controls and deceives you, and you let him because he tells you that it's what you're meant to do.

But you know deep down that he's wrong. I know you do. You wouldn't be here now if you didn't. He told you were to find me, didn't he?"

"I...I..." Indecision parades across her mother's face, aging her beyond her years. But the truth lurks in her eyes too. She knew Winter was going to be here today because he knew...and the only reason he knew is because he's been fucking stalking her.

"He tried to shoot your daughter," I say, twisting the knife a little deeper. It's cruel, but sometimes, cruelty is the best kind of mercy. It's the only kind that severs the chains dragging you under. "He shot an innocent man and allowed dozens of others to be trampled. And then he sent your daughter a letter threatening to kill her. Does that sound like a man of God to you?"

"He sent a letter?" she asks Winter.

"Psalm 94," Winter confirms, grimacing. "He twisted it all up, Mama. He said the pit had been dug and said I had to repent or dwell in the silence of death." She shivers. "He thinks he's God."

"Oh, Winter," her mom whispers, tears welling in her eyes. "What have I done? He's always been fascinated with you, always asks about you. I never should have taken you to that church."

I lower my gun as Winter flings her arms around her mom, pulling her into a hug. "You didn't know, Mama," she says fiercely. "You didn't know."

Her mom weeps silently, clinging to her daughter.

I shove my gun into my pocket, reaching for my phone to call Anderson.

"No!" Winter screams suddenly.

I glance up to see her horror-filled gaze trained over my shoulder. I drop my phone, grasping for my gun as I spin, putting myself between her and whoever the fuck is behind me. I already know I'm not going to get to my gun in time to save my own life, but at least I'll give her a chance to run. I'll give her a chance to save her own.

My life before hers. I can live with that.

My fingers close around my gun as my gaze lands on the man standing a few car lengths away, pointing a weapon at me. He's dressed in all black, a mask pulled down over his face. He doesn't move as he aims at me. Maybe it's the mask. Maybe he just doesn't give a shit. But he thumbs back the trigger as if he's done it a thousand times, his eyes completely cold and devoid of anything resembling remorse or emotion.

I love you, songbird. Close your eyes. I love you.

A gunshot rings out.

Winter screams, a haunted, painful sound.

I don't breathe, waiting for the pain to come. Except it doesn't.

What the fuck?

Brother Gibbs staggers forward a step, the gun falling from his hand. He collapses to his knees as the gun hits the ground at his feet. A wet spot blooms across his chest, spreading rapidly.

I rush forward, kicking the gun out of his reach before I spin toward Winter and her mom.

Her mom is holding a gun, her face contorted in grief.

Oh, fuck me. She shot him.

"Mama," Winter whispers. "Oh, Mama."

"I had to," her mom mumbles. "I had to. I had to."

I rush forward, prying the gun from her hands as shouts ring out in the distance, help finally coming. Far too late to help Brother Gibbs, I think. Not that I'm going to weep for the motherfucker.

"I decided something," Winter says hours later, curling up on my lap on the couch. She never managed to make it down the runway. Once Anderson arrived, we had ten thousand questions to answer. We only just got home a little while ago.

I have a feeling tomorrow will be a whole new shitshow. Once the press gets the story, they're going to lose their collective minds. Winter's childhood pastor tried to kill her, only to be shot by her mother. I don't think we'll ever really know why. The best we can guess is that he was obsessed with her and hated that she left the church to pursue music. When his letters didn't draw her back, he decided to up the ante. Regardless of whatever evil he had in his mind, there will be no stopping the story once it leaks. But for tonight, at least, Anderson and Riley are doing their best to keep it under wraps to give us one more night of peace.

I'm ready for whatever comes next. Bring it on. So long as Winter is by my side, I'm ready to face anything. I thought I was going to lose her today. Hell, I thought I lost myself today. But somewhere between arriving at that damn show and leaving, I found something I didn't expect. Forgiveness. Hope. Peace.

I couldn't save my team, and it's haunted me every day since. I've relived it over and over in my dreams, trying to will a different outcome into existence. But I can't change what happened. Part of me will probably always feel responsible simply because I survived. Because I wasn't fast enough to get there in time to warn them. But today, for the first time, their ghosts fell silent.

I learned to let go.

"What did you decide, songbird?" I ask, brushing my nose along her crown, breathing her in. I don't think I'll ever stop breathing her in or touching her, just to remind myself that she's still here and that she's safe. Christ, she's safe. Her mother saved her life.

She isn't going to face charges for killing Brother Gibbs, at least Anderson doesn't think so. His fingerprints were on the last letter. Anderson was working on getting an arrest warrant when Riley called him today. He's furious that his unmarked lost track of the bastard and allowed him to get so close to Winter. I am too. But what's done is done. He's not breathing now. He'll never threaten her or anyone else ever again.

I don't know if he truly intended to harm her or simply scare her. I don't want to know. It'll just drive me fucking crazy to know what he planned. So I'm just thanking God that the motherfucker can never hurt or threaten her or anyone else again. She's free, and so is everyone else he's ever hurt.

Her relationship with her mom is fragile, but I think they just might survive. Her mother made shit choices—there's no disputing that—but she loves Winter. Enough to kill to protect her. That's a pretty powerful indicator of just how deep her love runs. It gives me hope that their relationship can be mended.

"Fashion is far too exciting for me," Winter mumbles around a yawn. "From now on, I'm sticking to music."

My lips curve into a smile. "Good plan. I don't think I can handle another fucking day like today. It shaved years off my life."

"Aww, poor soldier," she croons, instantly solicitous as one hand skates down my body. Her lips land against my throat, gliding up toward my ear. "Maybe I should make it up to you."

"Fuck," I groan, arching into her touch when she wraps her hand around my cock through my jeans. "You keep touching me like that, I'm going to be fucking you on the couch."

"Oh, you mean like this?" She squeezes me, nipping my ear at the same time.

I growl, flipping her over beneath me. She lands on her back, her legs wrapped around my waist, smiling up at me like I hung the moon. Fuck, she's beautiful.

"Hi, handsome."

"Marry me," I breathe.

She blinks those amber eyes at me. "What?"

"Marry me, songbird. Let me put my ring on your finger and spend the rest of my life guarding your back," I murmur, brushing hair out of her face. "Let me spend the rest of my life adoring you."

"Yes."

"I wasn't finished."

"You don't have to finish. My answer is yes, Ronan. In this life and every other, it's yes."

"Jesus," I growl, claiming her mouth in a searing kiss. I pour everything into it—my heart, soul, and devotion. She mewls beneath me, clinging to my shoulders as she kisses me back with just as much passion, just as much need. "I love you, songbird."

"Good because you're stuck with me," she whispers against my lips as I drag her shirt up, eager to get her skin to skin. "I won't ever want this to end."

"Then it never will."

"I like this plan," she breathes, happiness shining in her eyes. "I just have one question."

"What?"

"Can I please have a phone again now?"

I lay my forehead against her chest, laughing quietly. "Fuck. I guess so."

Epilogue

Winter

<u>Five Years Later</u>

"Stop texting my wife," Ronan growls at Memphis, glaring at him across the aisle of the tour bus. "She's sitting right here, jackass."

"I know." Memphis smirks. "But watching that muscle in your jaw tick every time her phone dings is more fun for me."

I sigh, shaking my head as my phone dings again.

Ronan grabs it from the bench seat beside me and types out a response to Memphis before hitting send. Memphis's phone dings a second later and my drummer cracks up.

"Asshole," he mutters without heat.

Ronan just smirks and slides my phone into his pocket.

I swear, the two of them never change. It's been five years and Ronan is still as possessive as ever. Memphis thinks it's hilarious, so he goes out of his way to annoy my husband. Ronan doesn't really mind. He and Memphis are actually really good friends, but they love to pick at each other, especially when it comes to me.

"If you two don't behave, I'm telling Riley," I say.

Their smiles slide from their faces.

"Don't do that," Memphis complains. "She's evil."

"Memphis!" his wife says, smacking him on the arm. "Riley is not evil."

"Not to you. She loves you," he mutters. "It's the rest of us she terrorizes."

"If you guys knew how to behave, she wouldn't have to terrorize you," I remind him, not in the least sympathetic. Riley only terrorizes them because they cause trouble. They aren't nearly as bad as Kasen and Bentley, but they aren't exactly Boy Scouts, either. Especially Memphis.

"Uh, bullshit," Ronan says. "I behave and she still terrorizes me."

"That's because you're bossy and you annoy her," I say, shrugging. "You never do what she wants you to do. If you'd just cooperate once in a while, she wouldn't have to terrorize you."

"I cooperate," he lies.

Memphis snorts.

"What? I cooperate."

I pat his hand. "Of course you do."

He narrows his eyes on me, making me smile. He does not cooperate, and he knows it. When it comes to me, he's completely unreasonable. I'm the most overprotected country star on the planet thanks to him. I'm not complaining though. It's been five years since Brother Gibbs tried to kill me, and I'll never forget how terrifying it was or how helpless I felt. I'll never forget how it felt to see him pointing a gun at Ronan, or the gratitude I felt toward my mom when she shot him.

My parents and I are in a much better place today than we were back then. They don't always understand my life, but they try. They withhold judgment, at least. It's not perfect, but it's better than it was. We're a family again. Our kids have grandparents. For the last five years, I've been happy. Blissfully happy.

And so has Ronan. It hasn't always been easy for him. He still struggles sometimes, especially around the anniversary of that day. The nightmares always come back then. But for the most part, he's okay. He's forgiven himself. He's worked through as much of the trauma as he can. It'll always be with him in some ways. PTSD doesn't just disappear. There is no magic cure. But he isn't the same man he was five years ago, either. He's at peace now.

It's beautiful to see.

"Are you sad?" Memphis asks me.

"About the tour ending?" I shake my head, smiling. "Nope. I'm ready to be home with my babies again." This will be our last tour for a while. Now that our kids are getting older, I want to be home with them. I don't want them thinking it's normal to grow up on a tour bus. I want them to have a normal childhood doing normal things. And I want to be home with them.

I've spent enough of my life on the road. I've seen the world. I've played for millions. I'm ready to spend time with my husband and our babies, being a normal family. We haven't done much of that for the last five years. We've toured and lived the musician life. I'll always be a musician. That won't change. But I'm done with touring, at least for now.

Besides, I haven't told Ronan yet, but we have another little one on the way. I'm ready to raise at least one baby at home instead of on the road.

"It's about damn time," Memphis grumbles. "I'm getting too old to wake up in a different city every day."

"You're forty-two," his wife says, laughing at him.

"Exactly, angel baby. That's too fucking old." He picks her up, dragging her into his lap to kiss her.

"That's our cue to get the fuck out of here," Ronan mumbles to me, standing up.

I giggle, allowing him to pull me with him. "Goodnight, guys."

Memphis lifts a hand and waves but doesn't let Kylie up for breath.

Ronan pulls me down the narrow hall of the bus to our room and then closes the door behind us before pulling me into his arms. "Want to drown them out with some noise of our own, songbird?"

"Actually," I murmur, slipping from his arms. "I have something for you." I circle around the bed, pulling the pregnancy test and the little onesie out of the drawer where I hid them, and then cross back to him. "These are for you."

He takes the small bag, eyeing me curiously.

"Call it an end-of-tour gift," I say.

He grins before reaching into the bag to retrieve the items.

I watch with my teeth caught between my lip, my stomach fluttering anxiously as he unrolls the onesie. We intended to stop after Max was born two years ago. We both decided three kids was plenty. But we haven't exactly been careful lately, either. I think we both secretly wanted another one. I hope he secretly wanted another one too because it's too late to take it back now.

"Little Songbird," he reads before looking at the test. His eyes flash to mine. "Songbird, are you...?"

"Yes," I whisper. "We're going to have another baby, Ronan."

"Fuck," he growls, shoving the onesie and the test back into the bag. He tosses it toward the bed and then scoops me up into his arms. His lips come down on mine in a hard kiss.

"Does this mean you're happy?"

"Happy?" He pulls back to look at me, his forest eyes shining. "Baby, I'm fucking thrilled you're having another one of my babies," he growls, walking me backward toward the bed. "In fact, I'm going to show you just how thrilled I am right now."

"I love you," I whisper as I fall to the bed beneath him, my entire world exactly right. Just like it always is with him

"I love you too, songbird," he breathes against my lips. "Always have, always will."

Author's Note

Thank you so much for reading A Hero for Her. If you enjoyed this book, please consider leaving a review.

See you soon with Callum's Hope, a Silver Spoon Falls release!

Line of Duty

These front-line heroes have risked their lives and fought
for others in the **Line of Duty.**
Now they're fighting for the greatest gift of all … love.

Check out the series here: https://amzn.to/3QQj1nK
Feb 15 Fiona Davenport Owned by the Officer

https://www.amazon.com/dp/B0BR8P3QFZ
Feb 17 Kylie Marcus Claiming the Captain

https://www.amazon.com/dp/B0BRL62M7M
Feb 22 Nichole Rose A Hero for Her

https://www.amazon.com/dp/B0BR4N1FS8
Feb 24 Fern Fraser His Temptation

https://www.amazon.com/dp/B0BRNY6SWX
Feb 27 Alana Winters Homegrown Hero

https://www.amazon.com/dp/B0BRDKFC2N
Feb 28 Kat Baxter Lily's Forest

https://www.amazon.com/dp/B0BR4NP7VH
March 1 Elle Christensen In the Arms of a Soldier

https://www.amazon.com/dp/B0BRNRN6CL
March 3 Andi Lynn Falling for the Flier

https://www.amazon.com/dp/B0BRNN6S6L
March 5 Violet Rae Healing the Warrior

https://www.amazon.com/dp/B0BQZJ1L1N

Callum's Hope

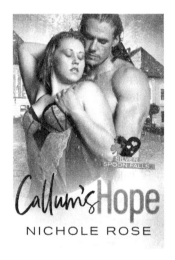

Finding love on St. Patrick's Day was not part of this bodyguard's assignment...

Callum

I've heard enough about the water in Silver Spoon Falls to know two things:

The people here don't joke about it. And I need to stay away from it.

But the luck of the Irish clearly isn't on my side.

Because I just got hired to protect the woman who bottles and sells it.

One look at Hope Byrne has me rethinking everything.

Starting with how soon I can make her mine.

There's something magical about this curvy little goddess and her fiery Irish spirit.

And I fully intend to break all my rules to claim her.

Hope

Thanks to the water, people in this town have always been lucky in love.

Why shouldn't others benefit too?

Giving them a little bit of hope makes me happy.

But someone is trying to destroy me and my business.

Hiring Callum Carmichael is my last chance to save it.

But I did not expect to fall for the grumpy giant.

Something about him makes my blood boil...and steam.

He's determined to knock down my walls.

I'm starting to think I want to let him.

If I survive the dangerous people determined to destroy me, anyway.

If you enjoy over-the-top bodyguards, fiery heroines, and steamy romance, you'll love this age-gap curvy girl romance!

Coming March 14th. Pre-Order Live!

Instalove Book Club

The Instalove Book Club is now in session!

Get the inside scoop from your favorite instalove authors, meet new authors to love, and snag freebies and bonus content from featured authors every month. The Instalove Book Club newsletter goes out once per week!

Join now to get your hands on bonus scenes and brand-new, exclusive content from our first six featured authors.

Join the Club: http://instalovebookclub.com

Nichole's Book Beauties

Want to connect with Nichole and other readers? We're building a girl gang! Join Nichole Rose's Book Beauties on Facebook for fun, games, and behind-the-scenes exclusives!

Follow Nichole

Sign-up for Nichole's mailing list at http://authorni
cholerose.com/newsletter to stay up to date on all new
releases and for exclusive ARC giveaways from Nichole
Rose.

Want to connect with Nichole and other readers? Join
Nichole Rose's Book Beauties on Facebook!

facebook.com/AuthorNicholeRose/

instagram.com/AuthorNicholeRose

twitter.com/AuthNicholeRose

bookbub.com/authors/nichole-rose

tiktok.com/@authornicholerose

More By Nichole Rose

Her Alpha Series
Her Alpha Daddy Next Door

Her Alpha Boss Undercover

Her Alpha's Secret Baby

Her Alpha Protector

Her Date with an Alpha

Her Alpha: The Complete Series

Her Bride Series
His Future Bride

His Stolen Bride

His Secret Bride

His Curvy Bride

His Captive Bride

His Blushing Bride

His Bride: The Complete Series

Claimed Series
Possessing Liberty
Teaching Rowan
Claiming Caroline
Kissing Kennedy
Claimed: The Complete Series

Love on the Clock Series
Adore You
Hold You
Keep You
Protect You
Love on the Clock: The Complete Series

The Billionaires' Club
The Billionaire's Big Bold Weakness
The Billionaire's Big Bold Wish
The Billionaire's Big Bold Woman
The Billionaire's Big Bold Wonder

Playing for Keeps
Cutie Pie

Ice Breaker

Ice Prince

Ice Giant

The Second Generation
A Blushing Bride for Christmas

Love Bites
Come Undone

Dripping Pearls

Silver Spoon MC
The Surgeon

The Heir

The Lawyer

The Prodigy

The Bodyguard

Silver Spoon MC Collection: Nichole's Crew

Echoes of Forever
His Christmas Miracle

Taken by the Hitman

Wicked Saint

The Ruined Trilogy
Physical Science

Wrecked

Wanton

Destination Romance
Romancing the Cowboy

Beach House Beauty

Standalone Titles
A Touch of Summer

Black Velvet

His Secret Obsession

Dirty Boy

Naughty Little Elf

Tempted by December

Devil's Deceit

A Bride for the Beast (writing with Fern Fraser)

Easy on Me
Easy Ride

Easy Surrender

<u>One Night with You</u>
Falling Hard
Model Behavior
Learning Curve
Angel Kisses

<u>Silver Spoon Falls</u>
Xavier's Kitten
Callum's Hope

<u>writing with Loni Ree as Loni Nichole</u>
Dillon's Heart
Razor's Flame
Ryker's Reward
Zane's Rebel
Grizz's Passion (coming soon)

About Nichole Rose

Nichole Rose writes filthy, feel-good romance for curvy readers. Her books feature headstrong, sassy women and the alpha males who consume them. From grumpy detectives to country boys with attitude to instalove and over-the-top declarations, nothing is off-limits.

Nichole is sure to have a steamy, sweet story just right for everyone. She fully believes the world is ugly enough without trying to fit falling in love into a one-size-fits-all box.

When not writing, Nichole enjoys fine wine, cute shoes, and everything supernatural. She is happily married to the love of her life and is a proud mama to the world's most ridiculous fur-babies. She and her husband live in the Pacific Northwest.

You can learn more about Nichole and her books at authornicholerose.com.

facebook.com/AuthorNicholeRose/

instagram.com/AuthorNicholeRose

twitter.com/AuthNicholeRose

bookbub.com/authors/nichole-rose

tiktok.com/@authornicholerose

Made in the USA
Middletown, DE
04 June 2023

31982165R00086